"Other Women is a sharp toothed and uncomfortable exposition of recklessness brought about by love and a weakness for beauty. I devoured this hypnotically intimate and vivid portrait of a woman's anger and appetite, her vulnerability and eventual power, found myself rapt and refreshed by its continuous surprising candor. A valuable and wholly original addition to the canon of literary other women."

Megan Nolan, Acts of Desperation

"In a voice that is just as powerful as it is vulnerable, Other Women perfectly captures what it's like to be young, bright, and sensitive, while finding yourself in love with the wrong person."

Juliet Escoria, Witch Hunt

OTHER WOMEN

a novel

nicola maye goldberg

Witch Craft Magazine

Cover and book design by Elle Nash

Cover image is "In Bed" by artist Federico Zandomeneghi.

Text set in Minion Pro.

978-1-7321920-0-3

For more information, email
witchcraftmag@gmail.com or visit us on the web at
http://www.witchcraftmag.com

For Kedian, as promised.

Now I am quietly waiting for
the catastrophe of my personality
to seem beautiful again,
and interesting, and modern.

-Frank O'Hara, "Mayakovsky"

I saw you for the first time at your girlfriend's birthday party last September, two weeks after I dropped out of school. In the hallway outside the apartment you shared with her off Franklin Street, a boy with long hair and ugly tattoos pushed me up against the wall, pinning me by my neck with his forearm.

I could have kicked him, maybe, but the thought didn't even occur to me. I was transfixed by the snake tattooed on his bicep, a skinny blue thing with bugged-out eyes. He looked as confused by the situation as I was, as if his arms had acted of their own accord.

After a few seconds he let me go. "Sorry for that act of violence," he said, and walked away.

If I was a different kind of person, I might have taken that as a sign from the universe that I should go straight home. But I fixed my hair and rang the doorbell. My hands were shaking.

Your living room was warm and loud and filled with smoke. Some people were squeezed onto a plump, cream-colored couch that looked as if it had been stolen from a retirement home. The rest were on the floor, some leaning languidly against the wall, others trying to make themselves comfortable, resting their chins on their knees as they muttered their contributions to the conversation.

There were newspapers and magazines on the coffee table, scattered among painted porcelain tea cups being used as ashtrays, empty cans of beer, and ratty copies of books by Badiou and Agamben. There was a Sol Lewitt print on the wall, some flimsy fabric draped over one window, and a couple half-dead potted plants giving off a rich, wet smell. You took my coat from me and placed it gently on the back of an empty chair. The slow, careful way you did this made me feel as if you were performing some sacred gesture, perhaps preparing me for a ritual sacrifice. You told me your name and kissed my cheek. I felt something inside of me flicker and go dark.

Kayla, who had invited me, was by the window, arguing with a tall boy, her posture as precise as a ballerina's. At the time, she and I were both working at a jewelry store near St. Mark's Place. She was friends with your girlfriend, Josephine, who came by the store occasionally. Once, she bought you a present there, a tiny gun made of gold on a long string of leather. I never saw you wear it.

Josephine waved to me from the corner of the room, where she sat cross-legged on the floor, cradling a sleepy, malnourished grey cat. She looked a bit like Monica Vitti, except happier. Her hair fell around her face, a pale fluttering curtain. She wore an amethyst on a black cord around her throat, which trembled slightly as she laughed.

I wanted to tell someone what had happened in the hallway, but I didn't know how to describe it. I wondered if the boy was a friend of yours, and if he was coming back to the party. Maybe I should have been afraid of him, but all I wanted to know was why he had done it. I wanted to ask him how it felt. All night, I watched and waited, but he never arrived.

During the party, I thought carefully about which possession I should leave at your apartment. My phone would have made things difficult for me. My necklace was too obvious. A hair clip wasn't urgent enough.

I sat on the floor of your bathroom and took everything out of my purse, deciding. The tiles of your floor were turquoise, and matched the cotton curtains that covered the small window - handmade, I realized, from the bits of thread dangling from the sides.

As I surveyed my belongings, I wished I had brought my umbrella, which folded up to be only a few inches long and could easily be forgotten on the floor somewhere. Eventually I took out one of my earrings – a silver hoop with glittery red beads dangling from it, a gift from my aunt – and placed it on the edge of the sink. The other I put in my pocket. I felt naked in a tiny, thrilling way.

I rummaged briefly through your medicine cabinet. Josephine was on the same brand of birth control that I was, I discovered, and she wore Clinique's Happy perfume. There was nothing I wanted to steal, though I did squeeze a bit of your toothpaste onto my finger, rubbing it on my tongue before I returned to the party. It tasted of real peppermint, healthy and expensive.

I called the next day. Kayla gave me your number.

"This is probably really weird," I told you, trying to keep my voice light and cheerful. "It has a lot of sentimental value, that's all."

"No, it's fine."

You sounded irritable. I'd waited until 1 o'clock to call, hoping to give you time to recover from your hangover. At the sound of your voice, I felt warm and tired with embarrassment.

"If you could just keep an eye out, that would be great. Maybe it got lost in one of the couches," I said, brightly. "But it's really not a big deal."

"I'll look, I promise." The sudden earnestness in your voice surprised me. Were you just trying to get me off the phone? I thanked you and hung up.

A few days later, I received my earring in an envelope with my name on it. Kayla must have given you my address. It was nice to meet you, said the note on the back of an index card. Your handwriting was as fastidious and elegant as a girl's.

At that time, I was still living in student housing. By some minor bureaucratic miracle, no one had bothered to make me leave. I shared an apartment with three other girls, all psychology majors. That, combined with the fluorescent lighting and linoleum floors, made the apartment feel like my own personal, wildly ineffective mental hospital.

One of my roommates, a tiny, energetic girl named Kathy, took a great interest in me after I dropped out. I wouldn't tell her why, which must have led her to believe it was something horrible and therefore fascinating.

She kept asking me to rate things of a scale from one to ten.

On a scale from one to ten, how stressed are you?

On a scale from one to ten, how much do you like yourself?

On a scale from one to ten, how satisfied are you with your life?

Or my particular favorite: On a scale from one to ten, how hopeless do you feel?

"Negative seven," I said, trying to confuse her.

"Christ, Kathy," I overheard one of the other girls, Gillian, say, after they thought I'd gone to bed. "Maybe she just doesn't like it here. Not everyone does."

Gillian was my favorite roommate. She had a really terrible eating disorder, which even Kathy didn't want to ask about. When I first met Gillian, at a party freshman year, she was glamorously thin, and I envied her immediately. Hers was a body that suggested discipline, restraint, self-control — all things I thoroughly lacked. By the beginning of sophomore year, she was so obviously, visibly sick that it seemed rude to mention it. She slunk around the apartment in expensive sweatpants, smoking cigarettes and cutting out pictures from Italian fashion magazines. On weekends we often watched television together.

Of the four of us, only Julia, an awkwardly tall girl from Westchester, seemed genuinely concerned with academics, and so I rarely saw her. She had a prescription for Xanax, which she sometimes sold to me for a very reasonable price. That was the extent of our friendship, which was fine with me.

That was the year I started pulling out bits of my hair. It began as a bad habit, an occasional accident. Then I started to leave it around the city, in the splintered edges of park benches, between the pages of newspapers left on the subway, around the doorknobs of diner bathrooms. I did it strand by strand, subtly, the way you pick flowers while leaving the bush intact. Someone must have seen me, someone must have noticed, but no one said anything. I was like Gretel, trying to find my way back to myself.

Shortly after I left school, I got a job at a very weird, hip jewelry store near Tompkins Square Park, which was where I first met Kayla. If I'd known her in high school, she would have terrified me. She was pretty, with deep-set hazel eyes and a large, expressive mouth, and almost a foot taller than I was. But she seemed to like me.

"High five," she said, when I told her I'd dropped out of school. "Me too."

Around noon, we started drinking, usually beer from the deli at the end of the street, sometimes gin out of the metal flask Kayla had decorated with stickers.

"Maude doesn't really care," Kayla said, referring to the elegant, mysterious owner of the store I never actually met. At one point she had been a slightly famous fashion model, but a few years earlier, she'd married a Russian stockbroker and opened up a jewelry store. "She just doesn't want to know about it, you know?"

Anyway, the job did not require a lot of brainpower. At the beginning, I hoped that I would get a lot of reading done. Though I faithfully brought *War and Peace* with me every day, I never made it past Pierre's duel.

My days took on a kind of rhythm, which, depending on my mood, was either comforting or excruciating.

Welcome

Hi

How are you

Have you been to our store before
I love your dress
If I could have you sign here for me please
I like your shoes
Have a good afternoon
Are you looking for anything in particular
Yes, there is a mirror right over there
Receipt in the bag
Thank you
Have a good evening
Hello

When the store was quiet, I talked to Kayla about her terrible boyfriends, the sketchy photographers who wanted her to model for them, and her deadbeat dad who called every once in a while to beg for money and/ or forgiveness. Her life seemed like a minefield of awful men, and I admired how gracefully she moved through it. "That's just what they're like," she said. "You can't take it personally."

A week after Josephine's party, you came to see me after work. Though I'd mentioned the store when we spoke at your party, I was genuinely surprised to learn that you had been paying enough attention to remember.

You waited outside while I locked up. My heart was a wild dog in a cage. It amazed me that I could still accomplish even the most basic of tasks— putting on my coat, opening up my umbrella, walking beside you, talking to you about your day.

You were dressed the same as any other vaguely hip white guy – jeans, leather jacket, ratty white converse, sunglasses – but on you it looked better, fresher, as if you were the first person in human history to ever wear that outfit, as if the city were full of cheap copies of you.

You told me you'd meant to go the to the Frick but you fell asleep on the train and ended up near Inwood Hill Park, where you'd wandered around for a couple hours, feeling like a ghost. In a grocery store you bought a large bag of some kind of Mexican candy which came in gold paper and tasted like powdered lemonade. I ate six.

"It's a nice park, actually," you said. "When the weather is nice, we should go."

You said this so easily, like we were old friends, like it made all the sense in the world for us to spend time together. It was very convincing. Or maybe I was just an easy target. I wanted to be convinced.

I told you that I was lonely, because almost everyone I knew in New York was a student. "All they talk about is, who's selling Adderall, which professor they want to fuck, etc. Which is fine," I said. "I just can't relate."

You nodded.

"Students can be tiring. You need to hang out with grown-ups."

"Is that what you are?" I asked, and you laughed. You were five years older than I was, which surprised me. I would have guessed we were the same age.

You asked me why I dropped out of school. I told you: "I thought I wanted to be a poet, but I really just wanted to be a poem."

"Everyone has that problem." You shrugged. "You just have to get past it. Turns out they're not as different as you might think."

I shook my head. "But I wanted to be the poet and the poem and the paper and the pen. When I sit in a class it's like someone is sewing up my lips."

That was probably the first thing I ever said that truly interested you. I could tell because you closed your pale eyes, like you were trying to really concentrate. This gave you a grave, almost ethereal expression.

It was bullshit, obviously. I dropped out of college for reasons that had very little to do with poetry. Sometimes I am able to really convince myself of certain stories I tell, of various motives I'd like to ascribe to myself. In this case I was simply lying. But I got addicted to that angelic look on your face.

One chilly weekend in November, Josephine went to Boston for a conference on free speech in the Middle East, and you invited me over. The plan, supposedly, was to watch Picnic at Hanging Rock, which you were surprised I'd never seen.

"You'll love it," you promised. "Lots of dead girls and white dresses. Very you."

You mixed gin and tonics, and we sat on your unmade bed and watched an episode of National Geographic about a woman who was in love with the Berlin Wall. She pressed her hands and face up to it like she was listening for someone on the other side. She said that the Great Wall of China was nice, too, but not as sexy as her husband.

"Oh my God," you said, delighted. "She's married to it." By the end of the episode — in which we learn that the woman has, due to extenuating circumstances, transferred her affection to a nearby garden fence — you were almost hysterical. To tell the truth, I didn't think it was that funny. I didn't feel sorry for this woman. I felt that I understood her perfectly.

Obviously we don't get to choose who we love, I thought. I was lying in an unmade bed that smelled of gin and soap and your girlfriend's perfume. All things considered, you can do much worse than a wall.

We stayed up until dawn. I watched the shadows of your eyelashes move rapidly across your cheeks. We got under the covers and you pulled me close to you, muttering something about goose-bumps. I tried to sleep beside you, but your heart beat so fast it bothered me. You couldn't believe how small I was, how cold.

In the morning you smoked a cigarette, pretending not to look at me. I dressed myself and went to run a bath. As I kneeled on the blue tile floor, checking the temperature of the water, I had a strange feeling, as if I was utterly pure, as if I had been scrubbed clean from the inside. There was no word for it: the only one I could think of was cauterized. The second I stepped into the bathtub it was gone.

As I was getting dressed, you said: this has to be a secret, and I nodded.

"No, really," you said. "It has to be."

I pinky-promised. It might have seemed silly, but when I was a kid one of my friends told me that if you broke a pinky promise God would hate you. I didn't believe that any more, strictly speaking, but I did attach great importance to that small vow.

Incidentally, I was supposed to see Tom that night. I completely forgot until the next day. He was one of the guys I'd been fucking on a semi-regular basis since I dropped out. Some of them, like Tom, had been my classmates, others were friends of friends who happened to be in the right place at the right time.

The sex was never that good, but of course the sex was never really the point. I needed a steady supply of boys to tell me I was desirable, or at the very least functional.

Every time someone so much as unbuttoned my shirt, I could not help but think: When did I learn how to do this? Wasn't I eight years old just a moment ago? And then of course I got so angry at whoever was touching me. How dare you? Can't you see I am only a child?

Anyway, I did not call Tom after that night, and he did not call me either, and I doubt he considered it any more of a loss than I did.

I knew Kayla might have information on you, but I wasn't sure how to ask for it. I was afraid to reveal anything. We were both still working at the jewelry store, and it was a slow day. I asked her about Josephine, instead.

"How do you know her, again?"

"I went to college with her brother. She used to come stay in our dorm sometimes when she was still in high school. It was really weird."

"Weird how?"

"Just, like, there was this sixteen-year-old girl running around," she said. "And no one fucked with her because her brother was around, but you'd see her at parties, this actual child, and the whole thing felt super creepy. But she's O.K. We don't hang out a lot but I think she's cool."

"She's really pretty."

"She is really pretty. All of his girlfriends are pretty in like, the exact same way."

"What way?"

"Uh, Blonde. Skinny. Private school. You know."

I nodded. Kayla went to private school too – the Queen of Jordan spoke at her graduation – but that seemed beside the point.

Kayla picked at a scab on her knee, considering. "I don't know," she said. "I feel bad for her, kind of. She loves him so much more than he loves her. It's super fucking obvious. But she could just break up with him. No one's forcing her to stay."

You didn't call me, and I didn't call you, and we didn't see each other again until a Christmas party at Kayla's ex-boyfriend's apartment.

Josephine was wearing a black velvet kimono embroidered with silver flowers and birds. Her cheeks were pink from wine, and she hugged me hello, wishing me Merry Christmas in a sing-song voice that made me want to strangle her. Your hand stayed on her waist as if it had been welded there. We said quick, disappointing hellos, your eyes not quite meeting mine.

I wanted to tell you: you can't make me the conduit for all your guilt. You can't look at me and see your moral shortcomings. You can't turn away so quickly.

I wanted to say: don't fuck me like you love me if you don't.

In January, Kayla asked me to move in with her. She lived with two other girls, both law students, in an apartment in Chinatown that looked like a fake hotel room from a porn video. It was poorly lit, very beige, and smelled vaguely of cat piss. The kitchen window looked directly down into the air shaft. "Perfect for jumping to your death!" she said, brightly, when I arrived.

A week later, the irritable Korean make-up artist who lived in the apartment next to ours moved out and was replaced with a man who had an unusually gruesome face. He didn't wear sunglasses, which I admired. I wondered if he wanted to scare people.

"Do you think he was born like that, or did something happen?" I asked Kayla in a whisper, after we passed him in the hallway on our way to work.

"Born like that," she said, with some authority. "If something had happened, the basic facial structure would still be in place."

She knew this because of a man she knew growing up, a friend of her father's who once threw a lit cigarette into the garbage by accident. The garbage caught on fire and the wind blew it into his face. Kayla said that used to be the most fucked-up thing she knew.

I got a job at a nursery school on the Upper West Side. The children were all delicately beautiful in the way wealthy children usually are, and they had names like Imogene and Artemis and Vladimir. My job was to play with them, and make sure they didn't hurt themselves, and to clean up after snack time (cheese in little silver packets, gluten-free crackers) and remind them gently, incessantly, to wash their hands.

I adored them all. It is hard not to adore beautiful children, and rich children are almost always beautiful. They adored me back, because children are much better than adults at reciprocating even the simplest kinds of love.

There was one girl named Daphne, who entered the classroom every morning, lay down on the floor, and wept. I kept thinking: you'd better get it together, kid. This is the best your life is ever going to be. This is the best anyone's life ever is, at this safe, clean place full of soft pillows and educational toys and people who are basically paid to love you. If you can't deal with this, there's nothing that is going to be O.K.

At my mother's request, I went to see a psychiatrist. It was either that, she said, or I had to come home. She didn't have to remind me that as long as she and my father were sending me money, my adulthood was only a legal technicality.

Initially, the idea seemed glamorous and exciting, and very New York City. I had never seen a psychiatrist before. In high school I had monopolized the time and energy of Ms. Gardiner, our overworked guidance counselor, who called me "sweetheart" and advised me to exercise more.

On a chilly Friday I took the 6 uptown, feeling terribly grown-up. You and your friends thought the Upper East Side was for old, bougie people, but I kind of loved it. When I was there I felt like nothing bad could possibly happen.

As I got into the elevator I was feeling so good I wondered if the psychiatrist herself would be redundant. Dr. Gordon's office was tastefully decorated, with framed Paul Klee prints, hardcover copies of books by Freud and Melanie Klein, and succulents in large ceramic bowls. She shook my hand warmly, and then said, "Before we get started, I'd like to discuss payment."

"Oh," I said. "You can bill my parents, I guess." I wrote down their address. Suddenly I felt like a kid sent to the principal's office.

"So," she said, smiling. Her hair, blonde tinged with

white, was held back by a large barrette, and there was a dot of shell pink lipstick on her teeth.

"What brings you here?"

"I drink too much. I'm always tired, even though I sleep a lot," I said. "And I don't care about my life." That seemed like a concise enough way to explain my problem, though, of course, the problem was that I couldn't explain it. Not really, not even inside my own head.

"Well, you care enough about your life to come here," she said. "That's a good sign."

I shrugged. "It was my mom's idea. She's worried about me."

"Why is that?"

"I dropped out of college."

"Oh." She scribbled something on a notepad. "And what are you doing now?"

"I work at a nursery school."

"How is that?"

"Fine. I like kids."

Another scribble. "Well, that sounds normal. Lots of people take time off school. Why did you drop out?"

"I was really sad."

"Why were you sad?"

"Everything was boring."

"Are you less bored now?" She looked up from her notepad. Her eyes were gray and her gaze was startlingly direct.

"Kind of. I feel more free."

More scribbling. I felt silly. This woman wasn't even pretending to give a shit about me – wasn't that her whole job? I was hurt by her lack of artifice.

I left her office half an hour later with a prescription for Lexapro and a newfound sense of despair.

During the second semester of my freshman year, a girl named Amanda Horowitz, a sophomore, jumped in front of a C train at West 23rd St. I saw pictures of the body online before someone took them down.

She was a junior, an English major, from Colorado. I didn't know her. We had one class together - Romantic Literature II – but I dropped it after a week, because it was at eight in the morning and the professor was not as attractive as I had heard he would be. I wondered if we would have become friends, me and Amanda. We probably had a lot in common.

In the photographs I saw of her, she was pretty in a delicate, generic way. She was a poet, or wanted to be one, anyway. I couldn't tell whether or not she was any good. Some of her friends published a chapbook of her work a couple months after she died. I tried to read her poems with a critical eye, but it was difficult. It felt like reading missives from a ghost. I tried to imbue my own poems with that mystical quality but of course it was impossible. They just sounded morbid.

I attended the memorial held by the school, hoping no one would notice that I had never even spoken to her. The memorial was so full that I suspected there were a lot of people like me; rubberneckers, people who, in the face of overwhelming grief, experienced what could most generously be called curiosity.

But my obsession did not end there. I copied her haircut, the bangs that ended just below my eyebrows. Lots of girls I knew had that haircut, but probably not for the same reason. To me, Amanda had found her place in the pantheon of dead girls: Ophelia, Sylvia Plath, Emma Bovary, Laura Palmer, Joan of Arc, Marie Antoinette. Before, she had been another college girl. Now she was a princess, a genius, an angel, a saint. And all she had to do was die.

I knew it was sick, but I was jealous of her. Even more jealous, because in death Amanda was pure, while I was full of these strange, ugly thoughts, which made being a normal person, or at least faking it, basically impossible.

I started to daydream about my funeral. I found it soothing, the way other girls liked to think about their weddings, or their dream homes. Whenever a problem presented itself, suicide seemed like a reasonable enough solution. When my parents asked me how I planned to support myself, I said that maybe I would go to law school, while in my head I decided which dress I wanted to be buried in. As my roommates watched the news, I perched on the edge of the sofa, dreaming of calla lilies and churches with stained glass windows. The world was a terrible place - who could argue otherwise? - and I was just relieved that I didn't have to deal with it for much longer.

That year, I got C's in two of my classes, a B in one, and failed the other. When I started my second year, I wasn't doing much better. A couple weeks into the semester, my advisor sent me a kind, concerned email, to which I never replied.

Instead I turned off my phone and walked all the way to the West 23rd street station. I swiped my card and stood by the tracks. The C train wouldn't arrive for another six minutes.

I watched a mother struggle to get her baby to calm down, hissing at it in a language I didn't recognize. A group of young businessmen were talking loudly and checking their watches. A teenage girl was using her phone as a mirror while she put on mascara so thickly that her eyelashes resembled spider's legs. A homeless man opened and closed his mouth but no sound came out. Please do not urinate on the subway platform, said a sign near my head. All along the platform were advertisements for insurance policies, gym memberships, and action films. I could have done it, but I didn't.

Most likely my vanity saved me. I didn't want to be a copycat. I stayed still when the C train passed, and then the one after that, and the next one, and the next. As I got out of the station I stopped and vomited into a garbage bin. I could hear the click of women's heels against cement as they passed me.

When I finally got back to my dorm it was dark outside. I stole some Xanax from Julia, ate a bowl of slightly stale Lucky Charms, and wrote an email to the Dean of Students. And then that was it.

You never once responded to me with blank stares or stunned silence or awkward, painful laughter. There seemed to be nothing I could say that would convince you I was too intense, too insane.

When I told you about the earring I left in your apartment, you laughed and said it was a nutty thing to do, definitely, but that you were glad I'd done it. I told you about my childhood obsession with Joan of Arc, of my totally irrational but somehow consuming fear of being burned at the stake, and you told me about a beautiful blue and white church in Mexico dedicated to Saint Lucy, who you said was your personal favorite. You promised, blithely, to take me there.

Once when we were having sex at my apartment, we kept almost falling off the tiny, unmade bed.

"What's wrong with us?" I laughed, and you said, "I've been wondering that for a long time," as if the same thing might be wrong with both of us. I didn't think that was true, but it made me happy that you might.

Once you told me I had a perfect mouth and I glowed for days. It was such a specific compliment, and you said it with deliberation, as if you had thought about my mouth for a long time before settling on the word "perfect." If you had ever told other girls they had perfect mouths - and I wasn't stupid, I knew you had - mine was still the most perfect. I don't know where this certainty came from.

After work, Kayla and I would come back to our apartment, get high and sit on the floor, and listen to songs sung by women with hearts even weaker than our own.

Weak hearts, but at least they made something out of it. I couldn't sing, couldn't paint, couldn't even write poems anymore.

What I did was draw, on old newspapers and flyers, whatever I felt like, pigs and mountains and babies with delicate faces. You enjoyed my drawings. You kept them folded inside your second-favorite notebook. You showed them to your friends, and didn't understand why I was angry. I thought you were making fun of me.

We never liked the same music. Once, when we were alone, I put on Etta James, and you just shook your head.

"These torch songs, they're just lullabies for ugly girls," you said. "They make it seem like not being loved is just as romantic as being loved."

"It isn't?"

"Well, what do you think?"

I shrugged. I didn't feel like I had enough data to say for sure, then.

You pulled me toward you. I noticed that your pants were too big. You looked ridiculous - why not just buy a pair that fit you? Maybe you thought they looked good.

Maybe Josephine did.

I was obsessed with the gap between your front teeth. It was not very large and I liked to think I was one of the few people who noticed it. It reminded me of how quickly your smile had turned into a kiss.

We measured our hands against one another. You squeezed mine tight and flipped me over. Around you, it felt terribly natural to be on my back. I was like a dog that was afraid.

I often heard girls, especially my old roommate Kathy, complaining that while the question between men and women had once been "how long do we date before we have sex?" it was now "how often do we have sex before we date?" An unfortunate casualty of the sexual revolution, it seemed, was that guys no longer needed to buy us dinner, or even really talk to us at all, in order to sleep with us. We had no bargaining power. I understood their frustration, and I was also keenly aware of my powerlessness when it came to romance.

But I still would have taken bad sex over a bad date, any day. A date entailed stiff, boring conversation over an overpriced meal, some half-hearted argument over the check, a lifeless kiss on the cheek at the end of the night. What was the point?

Sex, however, always revealed something weird and special about another person. I loved that. I barely remembered the guys I had sex with my freshman year, but I remembered that one had motivational quotes written on green index cards taped above his bed, that another shyly showed me his collection of throwing knives, that one kept kissing my forehead, a gesture that went from tender to creepy very rapidly, that one thought women looked sexier with bras on than off, that one just wanted to sit naked, together, and talk to me about how much he missed his high school girlfriend.

One wanted to be a surgeon, and the precise way he touched me made me feel as if I were about to be sliced open.

You called me late on a Wednesday night. I was about to go to bed, but instead I went to your apartment and helped you clean up half of a brown mouse that the cat had left on your pillow. Though it smelled like death itself I managed not to gag once, and afterward you turned on the television and offered me a beer.

The cat, a tiny Russian blue, belonged to Josephine, technically, but she loved you the best. She curled up against your arm while you were sitting on the couch watching The X-Files, and purred when your patted her tiny head. Her name was Mary-Louise.

"I love pets with really human names," you explained to me. "Someday I want a golden retriever named, like, Gregory."

"Christopher," I suggested. "Margaret."

"Richard."

"Eileen."

"Gloria."

"My mom's name is Gloria," you said.

"Really?"

"No, I'm just fucking with you." And then you took my face in your hands and kissed me. I was so happy, I thought my heart would die of joy. I really did.

As often as I was sure I saw you turning the corner as I approached, or in line for coffee, or disappearing into a crowded subway, I hallucinated Josephine. I mistook the faces of models in magazines for hers. All of a sudden New York was infested with tall girls with medium-length blonde hair. It was exhausting.

I frequently tried to get you to talk about her, to no avail. When I was around, you probably wanted to pretend she didn't exist. I understood this, but I wanted to know about her flaws. Maybe she made you feel small, with her beauty and her competence, and maybe it was my job to make you feel big again. There wasn't a lot of dignity in that, but I didn't care. I didn't care about integrity, or self-respect, or any of the things I knew I was supposed to want. I just wanted you.

Did that make me a bad person? Or at least, a bad woman? Probably. But I was under no illusions that I was good. Morally, I considered myself a C+, maybe a B-. People who think they're good are dangerous, because they can say to themselves: Oh, well, I am really good at heart, so it is O.K. if I do this terrible thing, because deep down I mean well. When I did the wrong thing, at least I knew that I was doing it. No one could accuse me of carelessness.

My mother insisted that I let her college roommate's nephew, a second-year medical school student, take me out for sushi. I wore a white sundress and sandals with ribbons that looped around my ankles.

"You look like a virgin sacrifice," said Kayla, pushing a lock of hair behind my ear. The restaurant, on 6th Street, had shiny green wallpaper and white linen tablecloths.

The medical school student was tall, even taller than you, and muscular, but he had a weirdly boyish face, which looked even stranger placed atop such a large body. He told me that he'd seen his first cadaver in class that week.

"A couple people got sick when they saw it," he told me. "Not a good sign, if you want to be a doctor."

I would have liked to say that maybe it was a good sign. That an aversion to death was something that I, personally, would want in a physician. Instead I asked: "What's the difference between a corpse and a cadaver?"

He looked puzzled.

"Nothing. They're both dead bodies."

"There must be a difference. Otherwise why have two words for the same thing?"

He laughed, not unkindly. "You're an English major, aren't you?"

"No," I answered, irritated. "I'm a drop-out."

To his credit, he did not ask me why I left school,

46

but rather continued to talk about his studies. When he ordered he pronounced the names of the dishes correctly, or at least they sounded correct to me. The waitress was unimpressed. At his suggestion I ate eel and some sour-tasting leaf. On a napkin I wrote: I miss you like bread misses the knife, like salt misses the wound.

More than three months after the first time we had sex, you met me after work and took me to a gallery in Chelsea. We walked through a giant maze made of wood and thick blue plastic. The maze was called "Mercury," which made it art, which made the whole thing feel slightly less seedy. Safely inside, you put your hand up my skirt, as certain and disinterested as though you were looking for your keys in the dark.

I read once that if you burst in on a woman undressing, she will instinctively cover a different part of herself, depending on which culture she is from. For instance, an American woman will have to choose between her breasts and her crotch, but will generally choose her crotch. A Finnish woman will turn her back to you. In Estonia, I think she will cover her feet. Somewhere — Laos? — it's the knees.

It made me think of Botticelli's Venus. It made me think, why not just cover your face? It made me think that there was no part of me that I was ready for you to see, no inch of skin that I didn't feel I ought to hide. There was no way that I could contort myself to avoid being emptied out.

Before I dropped out of school I took a class called Memorable Nineteenth Century Continental Novels. I met with the professor after class one day to talk about the essay I wanted to write. It was about *Madame Bovary* and *Anna Karenina*, and it had something to do with mothers and wives. When I told him my thesis, he grinned.

"Don't you think you're a little young for all this adultery?" he asked me. I must have blushed. He was probably right. But I hated the word cheating, because it suggested inflexible rules, winners and losers, some kind of final score. No one could ever write a novel about a betrayal that petty.

Some days I was so full of longing it was a wonder I could stand up straight, walk around. I became really tempted by Tolstoy's ideal of chastity. It made a lot of sense to me, philosophically. Maybe it would keep me out of trouble. Men and women ought to be educated in their homes and by public opinion to look, before and after marriage, on infatuation and the carnal love connected with it, not as upon a poetical and exalted condition, such as it is now considered to be, but as upon an animal condition, degrading to man.

And it's true, obviously, that sex ruins everything: friendships, bed sheets, Sunday mornings, New Year's resolutions. But I was nineteen years old, and anxious about missing out on certain opportunities. Besides, he was talking to men, not me.

In April, Kayla's mother, Caroline, came from Chicago to visit. She was pretty, like Kayla. Her voice was even louder and she moved slowly. She slept in Kayla's bed and Kayla slept with me in mine. It was nice, having a body beside me without any of the usual obligations.

We went out to dinner, the three of us, and Caroline got a bit drunk. She kept dropping her silverware on the floor, and a waiter kept silently replacing it. Jet lag, she said, which was obviously not true, but I wasn't sure if it was a joke or a lie. She told a story about Kayla as a kid, about the time two boys were suspended from kindergarten for fighting over who would get to marry her.

"One of them threw a rock at the other. Thank God his aim was bad. Can you imagine?"

Kayla scowled. "I remember that. It was so fucking stupid. They made you come pick me up from school, like I was the one in trouble, even though I didn't do anything. It was humiliating."

"Oh, come on. I took you for ice cream that day!"

"It was humiliating," Kayla repeated, but she was smiling.

As we were leaving, Caroline said something strange. She said: men destroy women. It's practically their job.

And then she laughed, and Kayla laughed too, but I stayed up all night thinking about it.

You told me about your ex-girlfriend, Elena. She was half-Polish, a couple years older than you. Another poet. She liked to be slapped around, you said. She wanted you to choke her.

"And did you?" I asked, calmly.

You shrugged. "Only because she wanted me to."

I didn't like imagining you like that, your hands around some other girl's throat. So I didn't.

Of all your friends, Peter was the only one I really got to know. The rest I avoided, partially because they frightened me —all those spoiled, stoned men with perfect teeth— and partially because I didn't know whether or not they could keep a secret. But I trusted Peter, because you did, and because he didn't strike me as the kind of person to find cheating particularly reprehensible.

He was rich, like you, and thin, like you, and had a strain of the same cruelty I had come to associate exclusively with rich, thin boys. You and Peter were in love with each other in the competitive, callow way young men often are. The way some boys played sports or joined armies, I think the two of you did drugs together as an excuse to touch each other's skin. I felt strange whenever I was in a room with both of you, like you wanted me to leave but didn't know how to say it.

The two of you had gone to the same terrible, expensive boarding school in Maine. I wanted to know more about it but you almost never talked about it, which of course made me want to know even more. You did tell me that one occasion, a teacher instructed each student to punch a mattress. Three kids to a mattress, you said. The idea was to get your anger out. After, the teacher had to drag the mattresses out back and burn them; they were so soaked through with blood.

Peter still sometimes wore the school's blue

sweatshirt—an act of defiance, I guess. When he was younger he was fat, you told me. I realized that must be why the sweatshirt was so huge. At your birthday party in April, he wore it with his tight pants and expensive, colorful shoes, like some kind of fashion statement.

I arrived at the party two hours late. I wanted to make you wonder if I'd show up at all. I wanted to make you anxious. When I got there someone handed me a drink almost immediately. Maybe I didn't eat very much that day, because it went to my head right away and I wandered through the rooms like a kid lost in a supermarket. I wanted to give you your present, a Fassbinder box-set. One of Kayla's rules was Never Buy Expensive Presents For Boys, which seemed sensible enough, but I couldn't resist. I opened the door to the bathroom without knocking.

You were doing a line off the top of the toilet and Peter was sitting on the floor, muttering about something. When you turned to look at me, blood ran down from your nose into your mouth. You pulled me in and closed the door behind you. When you kissed me I felt sick for just a second, and then it was like it always was: a feeling of floating away from myself, like I was ethereal, like I was invincible.

"I'll be right back," you told me.

Peter looked up at me, grinning. I think he liked being

your accomplice. He stared at me for a while, as if trying to determine whether or not I was worth the risk you were taking. As far as I know, he never told anyone what he'd seen.

Josephine's cat got fleas, and they bit my legs. During the night, I scratched right through the skin, staining your sheets. So I guess you could say I bled for you.

You told me that when you were eighteen, you tried to kill yourself.

How? I wanted to ask, but instead I asked, "Why?"

"I was bored," you said, smiling. A lie, obviously, but one so well-rehearsed it seemed rude to point it out.

"I think," you continued, "that suicidality isn't necessarily a pathology as much as a certain lens through which to view life." Your voice was so quiet. I wasn't sure I'd heard you correctly, but I was too shy to ask you to repeat yourself.

As a result, you told me, your mother sent you to a kind of rehab center in Montana. According to you it was the most beautiful place in the world.

"People have no idea," you said. "It's prettier than the South of France, than Greece, Barbados, anywhere." Having been to none of those places, I could only take your word for it.

While you were there, you met a girl who, as a child, had seen her father kill her mother with the claw end of the hammer.

"At that point in someone's life, it's like, just let her have the goddamn heroin, you know?"

"Yeah." To me, that sounded more than fair.

Even though you were sharing with me something intensely personal, it did not feel like intimacy. It felt like a test. Genuine moments of intimacy, I think, occur only by accident.

For instance: one morning, after you slept over at my apartment, I got ready for work while you were still sleeping. I dressed myself and brushed my hair as quietly as possible, trying not to wake you. But I could not resist kissing you goodbye, and as I did, you pulled me towards you, wrapping your arm around my waist.

"I like this sweater," you said. It was light brown, real cashmere, and easily the nicest thing I owned.

"Thanks," I said, absentmindedly. "I like it because it's so soft. That's how I buy clothes. Things that make me feel like I'm a stuffed animal." In fact, the sweater was my dad's, stolen from his closet during my most recent trip home.

"I'm the opposite," you replied. "I always buy really sturdy clothes, things that will last me until I'm dead." Your eyes weren't even open.

We kissed again, and talked some more, and ultimately I was only five minutes late for work. That exchange stayed with me all day, but it wasn't until months later that I realized why.

It was such a small, odd piece of information you'd given me, but there was a real possibility that it was something only I knew. Even though I knew you most likely forgot that conversation by the time you left my apartment, to me it was a real gift.

For my birthday, you took me to see La Traviata, and though we had to stand for the whole thing I adored it. That was all I wanted then: to die beautifully, in a silk dress, surrounded by everyone I loved, singing and apologizing.

("You look like a porcelain doll," you said to me, once. "But isn't the best part of a porcelain doll smashing it on the ground?" You said that, too. You really did! And how did I respond? I probably laughed, and changed the subject. It makes me sick to think of it, now.)

I loved it when you slapped me during sex. It was my idea. At first you were nervous you would leave a mark, but I promised you I didn't bruise easily. I liked the way you caressed my face just before, the insane tenderness of it.

Before dropping out, Kayla had spent two years at SVA studying illustration. I asked why she left.

"It sucked and it was expensive," she said, which sounded reasonable enough, except that I strongly suspected it had something to do with a boy named Alexei, who I sometimes saw at parties, or sneaking out of our apartment early in the morning. He was from Lithuania, 6'4, with blue eyes and extraordinary cheekbones. His nose and lips were very thin, arranged in a perpetual sneer.

"Hot in a scary kind of way," was how Kayla described him, and I could see that he was the type of guy who could ruin your life without even trying. It is terrible to love someone cruel. It suggests something rotten without yourself. After you have loved someone cruel, no one else will do.

"Bad boys are exhausting," Kayla told me, after she and Alexei broke up for what she swore was the final time. "They're just garden variety sociopaths with decent wardrobes. And girls are so dumb about them. It's like, buy your own goddamn leather jacket and move on with your life." She sounded confident, but I don't think either of us were convinced.

She poured herself another drink. Kayla only drank alcohol straight, claiming that mixed drinks and chasers were a waste of money and calories. I picked up the habit, and when we drank together, sitting on the floor of her room, our throats burning, I liked to think of us as hard-boiled detectives, or possibly cowboys, discussing the sorry state of the world in some glamorously seedy bar, perhaps in Los Angeles.

I liked to think that when we were talking about sex, we were really talking about love, and that when we were talking about relationships, we were really talking about being human. But in all likelihood we were just two smart girls marveling at our own stupidity.

Once we were having sex and you bit me, hard, just below my collarbone. A couple days before you asked if you could, and I said no. Your eyes stayed open. I began to cry. You sat beside me, still naked, your knees pulled up to your chest. "Are you alright?" you asked, pathetically.

I continued to cry. I put my underwear back on. I got up and looked in the mirror, at the vague outline of red. If I'd walked into a door it would have looked the same.

"I'm so sorry," you said.

"It's fine," I said.

"I feel like I raped you," you said.

"Don't be ridiculous." I sat down next to you. I felt the coarse, cold hairs of your thigh against mine. "It's fine. Just don't do it again."

"I feel horrible. I feel like I should die."

If I were to repeat those words to anyone, they would sound completely absurd, even for a poet. But when you said it I knew you meant it. I held your head in my arms.

"It doesn't matter, it didn't even hurt," I said. "I only cried because I was surprised."

That was a lie, but I didn't cry because of the pain, either. You humiliated me. You did it without even trying. As I held you, my shame grew and grew. I knew that there was nothing I wouldn't do for you. I knew that there was nothing I wouldn't let you do.

I think if you wanted me less, you might have loved me more.

On the last night we spent together, I kept drifting in and out of sleep. I was dreaming that I was somewhere else: my high school cafeteria, a hospital waiting room, Mars, a movie theater. Every time I woke I was so happy when I realized I was still next to you. Your bed, with its dark blue sheets, the steady hum of your air conditioner, an empty bottle of Gatorade on top of a pile of books, the heap of clothes on your floor, the dirty towel draped over a chair. This was heaven to me. Every second I spent with you felt impossible and precious, liable to be the last.

When I received a card in the mail that informed me of your engagement, my first thought was how weird and old-fashioned it was. Thick, expensive cardstock, dark blue lettering, sealed with a gold sticker. It must have been Josephine's idea to send it. Of course you were a pathetic coward for letting me find out like that, but the anger didn't come until later.

First I cried, stupidly, hysterically, like a child. Then I burned the card, using a $7.99 lavender-scented candle I bought from the nearest CVS. It was a dramatic, satisfying gesture, but when it was over, I still felt like I'd been kicked in the stomach.

I wanted to go to your engagement party, really I did. I had a fantasy of showing up looking tragic and beautiful, making you regret your decision, making you realize the damage you had done. Kayla convinced me not to.

"There's no best-case scenario," she told me. "There is no way it won't be terrible. It's just, like, what kind of terrible will it be?"

At first I was annoyed at her advice, which I found condescending. But I was grateful for the excuse. After all, I am a coward, too.

I even lent Kayla a skirt, a black, silky thing that looked slutty on me but gorgeous on her. Did you recognize it?

I dreamt that every hair on my body was a small blue flower. Someone plucked them one by one. It was you and it was not you. I woke up too early. It was still dark outside.

Like everyone in the whole world, I had romantic notions about New York City before I moved there. After a week of men jerking off next to me on the subway, and walking past piles of trash taller than I was, I was more than ready to admit defeat. I'd settled in, the way most people do, but around the time we met, I'd started waking up, often from vague nightmares, at four or five in the morning, and going for walks. The early morning was the only time New York felt the way I'd hope it would: glittering with promise, entirely open to me.

The morning after I learned you were getting married, I woke around 5 a.m. I was starving, and none of the food in the refrigerator was mine. I pulled my coat over my nightgown. The nightgown was pink and lacy and only partially see through, so I sometimes wore it as a dress, hoping to look chic in a disheveled sort of way.

There was a 24/7 supermarket one block from my apartment. I bought a box of blackberries, a sleeve of crackers, some almonds and a packet of potato chips. As he finished packing my groceries into a paper bag, the cashier looked at me through sleepy eyes and said, almost as a goodbye, "Pretty girl."

Whenever someone told me I was pretty, I longed to say "I know." Not because I really felt that I was, but because I wanted to see what it would be like to be so confident. I had an idea that it might be attractive to men. Or maybe it would repulse them. I never found out.

I muttered "Thank you," and left.

I went home. I tried to sleep, but couldn't. I tried reading, watching television, doing the dishes. I even offered to take our neighbor's decrepit German Shepherd for a walk. I hadn't seen Kayla all day. While I was waiting for her I drank cheap bourbon straight out of the bottle. I tried to imagine myself as Bukowski or someone like that, but I was unable to fool myself into feeling glamorous. By 8 p.m. Kayla still wasn't home. I wondered, dully, if she was avoiding me. I went into the bathroom and made myself throw up as much of the bourbon as possible, and then I laid on my bed. It was disgusting, and it made my throat hurt, but it also made me feel calm and pure.

If you and Josephine were normal people, I could have tortured myself daily by stalking the two of you online. But you, of course, were too cool to even have a Facebook profile, and Josephine was too classy to post pictures of anything except for the occasional panoramic view of the coast. Once, she posted a photo of two large blue paintings side by side in what must have been a gallery or museum. In one, I could see your reflection, slightly hunched over. "Object of desire," she'd titled the picture.

There were times when I'd felt sorry for Josephine but when I saw that photo I immediately longed to take a cab over to your apartment to strangle her. It was embarrassing, that kind of jealousy. It made me hate myself even more than I hated her, even though you were the one who deserved it. I saw that fucking picture in my dreams.

In a heroic attempt to cheer me up, Kayla took me to a bar in the Village. She was trying to have sex with a guy whose band was playing there. The band was terrible, and this guy was almost definitely terrible, and I wished so badly I had something better to do.

I was surprised to see Tom, the boy I had been sleeping with before we met. He was wearing a blue button-down shirt, and smelled of soap and beer. We were standing right next to each other, but in the throng of people he didn't seem to notice me. Or he was pretending not to.

It occurred to me that I had sex with people I didn't care about, and who didn't care about me, in hopes that I would learn something about myself in the process. I stared at Tom, in his too-big jeans and his stupid fucking shirt, and wondered how I ever thought he had something to teach me.

A few feet away, Kayla was dancing by herself, joyful and absurd. Men were watching her with interest, with contempt, with longing. Where did you learn to do that? I wanted to ask. How did you learn how to be who you are?

Three shots of tequila later, I tapped Tom on the shoulder. He smiled convincingly and gave me a hug.

"How have you been?" he asked me.

"I'm good! I'm really good. I haven't seen you in so long."

"I know! I was wondering how you were."

"Same. How are you?"

"I'm great."

We were lying to each other with considerable enthusiasm, so I wasn't surprised when he asked me if I wanted to go outside for a cigarette, nor was I surprised when he kissed me, but I was a little taken aback when, five seconds later, he pulled away from me and put his face in his hands.

"I'm sorry," he said. "I have a girlfriend. I feel awful. I'm sorry."

"Do I have a fucking sign on my forehead?" I muttered.

"What did you say?"

"Nothing." I put my arms around his neck. "It doesn't matter. I don't care." I didn't.

"I do," he said, and pushed me away, probably harder than he meant to. I started to cry, not out of pain, but surprise. He looked stricken. People walking by glared at him but kept going. I thought he would draw me to him, to comfort me, or at least to keep me quiet, but he disappeared back inside. I threw my empty glass against the sidewalk. A thrill went through me as it shattered, shards of glass catching the glint of the streetlights, exploding like stars across the dirty pavement.

A man in a suit stopped and put his hand on my shoulder.

"Miss, are you alright?"

"Oh, fuck off," I said, not looking at him.

"Fucking bitch," he said, and kept walking. I watched him disappear around the corner and cried some more.

Kayla should have been wondering where I was. I checked my phone. No new messages. I thought of her dancing, her body made of equal parts flesh and sound. How could I interrupt that?

I walked ten blocks away from myself, biting my wrist. *I'm losing it*, I thought, and that thought frightened me so much that I got even more panicked, even more afraid. I walked and I walked. I wasn't in a nice area, I registered, vaguely. I wasn't wearing a coat.

It was getting dark. Groups of men spilled out of clubs and delis and subway stations. I was two girls at once then. The one who was insane, and the one who was following her, struggling to keep up, saying why don't we turn around now, why don't we just go home. Eventually that girl grabbed the other one by the arm and dragged her to the bus stop, where they both sat for a while, saying absolutely nothing.

I decided to go to Berlin.

There was a family, the Herzfelds, at the nursery school looking for an au pair. I guess because I had exactly one semester of college German, the school's director suggested me. They had two kids, a three-year-old named Lily and a fifteen-year-old named Sophie.

I went to the Herzfelds' apartment to talk about arrangements for Berlin. They were in the process of packing up, so the whole place was a mess, but still beautiful. The apartment had dark wood floors and white walls and so many windows. Just imagining living there made me happy.

Henry Herzfeld did something Very Important at a Very Famous Corporation. My dad had actually heard of him, weirdly enough. Until a few years earlier, his wife, Charlotte, had been a dancer. Even if she hadn't told me that, I would have guessed. She had a dancer's posture, and dancer's legs. Even the way she shook my hand made classical music play in my head.

In jeans and a t-shirt, I might have mistaken her for someone my own age, but she was wearing a black linen dress and tiny diamond earrings that caught the light whenever she moved her head. She even smelled expensive.

Charlotte made Oolong tea and the three of us sat in the kitchen and talked. Her soft voice made me think of ballet slippers and piano lessons and trips to the seaside, of a childhood I craved, even when I was still a child. From their kitchen I could see the East River, so beautiful it distracted me.

Their current nanny brought Lily home from a play-date around three o'clock. To her credit, Sophie was very sweet with Lily, who was her half-sister. She put Lily on her lap and fed her half of a sugar cookie. Charlotte watched them from across the table, her face totally serene.

The whole thing felt like being in a dollhouse or the set of a television show; unreal and kind of invasive. I felt like any second Charlotte would realize I was there and kick me out. But she seemed to like me. So did Lily; she was a cute kid, she probably liked everyone.

Sophie hadn't made up her mind yet. It was funny. She seemed so much older than I was when I was fifteen, in the way that city kids often seem older than they really are. Sophie was the kind of pretty, intense girl who would have terrified me when I was in high school. I had no idea how I was supposed to exercise any kind of authority over her.

The next day Charlotte took me with her as she ran errands to prepare for Berlin. We went to Bloomingdale's and I helped her pick out a new suitcase for Sophie, and then CVS to get my passport photos taken, and then we took a taxi to the passport office, where we stood in line for what felt like forever. She gave me some cash to go get us both coffee, and I did, but a security guard made me throw it out. Fascists, Charlotte whispered in my ear.

Charlotte said she had to go grocery shopping, and I wasn't sure whether or not she meant for me to come along, but I had nothing else to do. We went to a fine food store on 2nd Avenue.

A lot of the things there sounded made-up to me: pink Himalayan salt, music paper bread. A bag of almonds cost three dollars. I watched Charlotte inspect French yogurts in little glass jars.

The sight of meat, wrapped tightly in plastic, made me think of a dead girl in a raincoat, and I told her I felt a little sick and that I was going to stand outside. A few minutes later she brought me a sugar cookie in the shape of a pig. The icing was pink and it had a tiny dot of dark chocolate for the eye.

Kayla threw me a goodbye party. She invited everyone she knew, so I ended up meeting a lot of people for the first time. Everyone had an opinion about Berlin they wanted to share. The consensus amongst these strangers was that I would love it.

A sickly, elegant girl with dozens of piercings put her pale hand on my shoulder: when you grow up in, like, Bumblefuck, U.S.A., you dream about going to New York City. When you grow up in New York City, you dream about going to Berlin.

"I'm from Massachusetts," I said, and she looked disappointed.

Around 11 p.m. I spilled rum and coke on my dress and went back to my room to change. When I came out, Peter was in the hallway swaying a little. It was the first time I'd ever seen him without you, and it felt, for a moment, like a consolation prize. He said he had to be somewhere and he'd just come to say goodbye.

He hugged me for a long time and I thought he was going to kiss me, but either he changed his mind or I was imagining it all, because he didn't. I realized after he left that I didn't even have his email address. It was totally possible that I would never see him again. Not that it was such a huge loss, but it scared me, how easily people just float away from each other, and how often.

The Herzfelds lived in Prenzlauer Berg, in a big apartment really close to the Rykestrasse synagogue. It was a beautiful building, all yellow and white, with a nice courtyard. I had a small room to myself with a comfortable bed, a framed Klimt print and a window that didn't open.

Of the five of us, Henry, who grew up in Freiberg, was the only one really fluent in German. Charlotte said she had a reading ability but she got very flustered whenever she asked for directions or ordered off a menu.

For the first week we were there, Sophie was mostly silent. Lily would attend a German kindergarten so she could learn the language while she was still young, when it's easiest.

"Only for Americans is being bilingual such an accomplishment," said Charlotte. "Everywhere else in the world it's a prerequisite." Sophie was going to the American school.

I saw Henry maybe twice in the weeks since we arrived because he worked so late. He looked exactly the way I'd expect a hedge fund manager to look, except paler.

The girls started school in September. Charlotte was still looking for a job. She had friends who worked at an English-language magazine but she said she'd rather just do research for her next book. She said it so casually, like she was considering switching to a new brand of laundry detergent.

I sent you an email. I couldn't help myself.

Today I went grocery shopping and I swear I saw the Berlin version of you. He was dressed all in black, buying nothing but hard liquor and cat food. I hate grocery shopping here because the store closest to our apartment is underground but also super brightly lit, which makes it look more or less the way I'd imagine hell, except with a much wider selection of candy. Since arriving, I almost only eat German chocolate and tangerines. The pockets of all my clothes smell sweet.

On the day before school started for the girls, Henry took all of us to dinner at a really nice restaurant in what used to be a Nazi bunker. Another thing you'd like about Berlin: everything used to be something else. The Mohrenstrasse U-Bahnhof is made out of red marble from Hitler's chancellery. I read about a youth hostel that used to be the Nigerian embassy.

The restaurant was decorated with a lot of warm light and red fabric. Sophie sulked and Lily spilled her Shirley Temple on my dress. Henry and Charlotte must have been fighting about something, because they barely looked at each other the whole meal.

Charlotte got a little drunk. With her cheeks flushed she looked so much like a porcelain doll. It was occasionally shocking to me that she had children, a job, a real life.

The whole experience was awkward but I had a nice time anyway. I liked the Herzfelds best when they seemed to forget that I was there, when I got to see them the way they really were. Other people's families are usually such closed circuits. Sometimes when I was with them, I felt like a spy.

Charlotte and I took Lily to her first day of kindergarten. The school was in a cute brick building, just six blocks from our apartment, next to a water tower that used to be a Gestapo torture chamber. I knew that because there was a sign in front of it that said so.

After settling her in, we went to some sort of administrator so that Charlotte could explain who I was, and tell them not to call the police if I came to take Lily home. She started off in halting German but after about thirty seconds the woman put her out of her misery and switched the conversation to English. Charlotte and I had to sign a few forms and then we were free to go.

She took me for coffee in a café that had a patio in the back, covered by a pergola strung through with fairy lights. I'd been getting stomach aches from all the coffee I was drinking so I ordered tea instead. It came with a tiny sugar cookie in the shape of a star. The waitress had short black hair and a tattoo of two mermaids kissing on her upper arm.

Charlotte sighed as she stirred milk into her coffee. "Sometimes when I walk around and overhear all these little children speaking in German I get envious. I think, 'you're four, how do you know when to use the dative?'"

"I know what you mean," I said.

"My German used to be much better," she told me. "I'm out of practice. My French is still excellent, but not

79

very useful here."

"No, I guess not."

"Maybe we should go to Paris. Even just for the weekend." Charlotte said, wistfully, and I wasn't sure if we meant the family, or - maybe, maybe - the two of us.

"That sounds nice," I said, uncertainly.

"Doesn't it? You seem like someone who would do well in Paris."

I had no idea what that meant, but I gathered that it was a compliment.

"I read your poem," Charlotte told me.

"Oh?"

"Yes. Before we hired you. I googled you, you know, to make sure you weren't a terrorist or a crazy person. Henry wanted to get the firm's investigator to do a proper background check but I said, stop being so paranoid. Anyway, I found your poem. The one that won a prize?"

"Oh, yeah," I said, as if I hadn't known exactly what she was talking about. I'd written the poem when I was in eleventh grade, and my teacher sent it to a contest for young writers. I received $200 and was invited to an award ceremony at Carnegie Hall, which was, easily, the best day of my life. "That one."

"I thought it was beautiful, really." She put her hand flat against her chest, a gesture I would have taken as mocking if it had been done by anyone else. "That's part of why I hired you, you know."

"Wow. Thanks." This seemed like a pretty stupid way to choose someone to whom you will entrust your child's safety, but what did I know.

"That's what you were studying, right? At school, before you took time off? Poetry?"

"Well, English, technically. But yeah."

"And have you been writing here, in Berlin? I want to make sure you have time to write."

"A little. Bits and pieces."

I didn't tell her that I hadn't written anything in months, aside from a few emails to you, which I mostly restrained myself from sending. It seemed unlikely that I could write one truly excellent poem and then not a single one after that, but that's what it looked like.

"You're very talented. It would be a shame to waste your time here."

I was tempted to say you know you're paying me to be here, right? I wasn't sure where my irritation came from. Charlotte was being nice, and as far as I could tell, sincere. Maybe I was just tired of people telling me I was wasting my potential. I had my own mother to do that.

I told her a story about a babysitter I had when I was eight or nine. She had red hair like mine, so I actually looked more like her than like my mother, and people often assumed I was her daughter.

She took me to gymnastics once a week, until once when my mother had the day off work and said she'd take me instead. This babysitter begged my mother not to reveal who she was-- all the teachers and all the other parents and the gym thought I was her daughter.

Charlotte laughed, then sighed deeply.

"People sometimes think Sophie is my biological daughter, and sometimes they think she's my sister. I don't know which one she hates more."

"You two seem to get along pretty well," I said. "That's a tough age. I was a total monster when I was fifteen."

"Me too! It's scary, learning how to be a woman. And even harder when you don't have someone to guide you. I mean, I try, but she doesn't want me to, so what can I do?"

"I don't know. I guess what you're doing now is good. Giving her space."

"Greer-- that's Sophie's mother - lives in some sort of women's commune in Iowa. Or Indiana? She rides horses and prays all day. I've seen pictures. It looks very beautiful. Sometimes I'm jealous." She laughed.

"I'm scared of horses," I said, stupidly.

"You know what? Me too."

"They're just too big."

"I agree! I don't know whose idea it was to domesticate them. I think they ought to be left alone, like lions."

"And they smell like their own shit," I added.

Charlotte wrinkled her nose, and I was embarrassed for swearing.

"Anyway, I met Henry about a year after the divorce. He was having a hard time. He didn't know how to take care of himself. He and Sophie ate takeout every night. They barely spoke to each other. It was so sad." She shook her head. "I met Henry at a grocery store. He was so tired, so out of it, that he walked right into me with his shopping cart, and I fell and sprained my wrist."

"What!"

She laughed. "It has a happy ending, though. He came with me to the hospital. He felt so bad! He wanted to pay for everything, and I said—I couldn't believe myself— why don't you take me out to dinner instead?"

"That's cute," I said, a little uncertainly. Charlotte seemed to think it was a sweet story. I thought of my own parents, who met at a Laundromat. Charlotte and Henry's story was definitely more romantic than that. (And what about you and Josephine? I wondered where the two of you ranked.)

Charlotte dropped another sugar cube into her coffee. "My mother told me that men can be good husbands or good fathers but never both, and most are neither. She told me to make a choice and live with it. But she was wrong, because Henry is both. Don't you think?"

I thought that if she had to ask my opinion, it probably wasn't a good sign. But from what I had seen so far, Henry seemed relatively competent in both roles. I wondered what category you would fall into: good husband, good father, or none of the above. You weren't much of a boyfriend, which didn't bode well.

The idea of you having children with Josephine - with anyone! - was too bizarre and too painful to bear, and so I turned my attention back to Charlotte.

"Yes. You all seem very happy together."

Charlotte beamed.

"You know, it's so rare. And I see so many of my friends settle. These smart, gorgeous women, they marry men who are not worthy of them, because they're scared to wait too long. They think that's the best they're going to get. And it's just so sad to me, because there are truly good men out there! You just have to be patient."

I wanted to tell her all about you, to ask her advice, but I was afraid what she might think of me.

After school, I took Lily to the park near our apartment. She fell off a swing and skinned her knee. She cried a lot, more out of surprise and humiliation than pain, and it was terrible to watch. It took me a few seconds to realize that the crying came from the child that belonged, at least for the afternoon, to me. My immediate thought was actually: someone should do something! I picked her up and kissed the wound, and she calmed down immediately. It occurred to me that the widespread practice of kissing children's injuries is probably unsanitary. I carried her on my back to the nearest drugstore and let her pick out the kind of Band-Aids she wanted.

As she deliberated between Hello Kitty and Cinderella, I thought about the time I fell down the stairs outside your apartment. I was a little drunk, but mostly I just wasn't paying attention to where I was going. It really hurt and I had to make a sincere effort not to cry in front of your friends. We were all on our way out to go see a movie. You told them to go on without us. Josephine kissed your cheek before she left.

You half-carried me back up the stairs. "Knees are like foreheads," you told me. "They bleed a lot more than you'd expect."

You didn't have a first aid kit so you folded up some toilet paper and held it against my leg as I lay on the carpet. We stayed like that for a long time. I thought you might kiss me, but you didn't. We missed the first fifteen minutes of the movie, a very bleak, loud action film about WWII that I didn't enjoy at all.

For the rest of the night - for the next few days, really - I was acutely aware of the place where the blood had been, of a flickering ache that appeared when I walked. It was embarrassing, how happy it made me.

The better I got to know Charlotte, the more I thought it was cruel of Henry to bring his family to Berlin. She hated it there. She pretended not to. She was always going to gallery openings and interesting restaurants and plays where everyone in the show was naked. But she had no friends there, and though she technically had a job I never saw her do any work. He had taken her away from practically her whole life.

Henry's family hated her. They didn't even bother to pretend that they didn't. Henry's parents came for dinner and they spoke in German the whole time. For a while Henry kept translating for her but he gave up quickly and she spent the rest of the dinner staring at her food like she was hoping it might jump up and attack her. The awful thing about that was I knew Henry's parents spoke English, because they interrogated Sophie for about an hour on her schoolwork. Sophie, true to form, gave them nothing. It was the first time I'd ever seen her and Charlotte on the same side. Around 8 p.m., I took Lily to have a bath and go to bed.

I felt very protective of that whole family, except for Henry, who, frankly, I didn't like at all, even though I barely saw him. Even Sophie seemed lost, much quieter and paler than when I met her in New York. She hadn't quite warmed to me yet, but I was hopeful. Lily was so sweet, in the way that most five-year-old girls are, but I adored her particularly, probably because I felt responsible for her.

The person I worried about most was Charlotte, which I knew was weird, and maybe even unfounded, but you should have seen the way she walked around, like she had no skin on. Every siren, every half-blind homeless man, every uneven cobblestone seemed to wound her.

Henry and Charlotte threw a dinner party. Ostensibly they were celebrating Henry's birthday, but I had a feeling the real reason was to give Charlotte something to do. There were people in and out of the apartment all day--caterers, florists, Turkish men delivering what appeared to be several hundred tables and chairs. It seemed very overwhelming, but Charlotte was totally calm, the happiest I'd seen her since we got here.

I offered to take Lily to the park, for my sake as much as for hers. I helped her to build daisy chains, which was a bit beyond her current motor capabilities, but she seemed enthusiastic anyway. By the end of the afternoon she had six or seven draped over her head and neck and little wrists.

A thin, elderly woman in an elegant blue coat approached us, with a rather wolf-like dog at her side. Both of them made me instantly nervous, but Lily placed her small hand in front of the dog's nose, and when it licked her, she giggled and placed a daisy crown on its large gray head. The woman smiled at me, and we spent the next few minutes watching Lily play with the dog, scratching behind its enormous ears and burrowing her face in its fur. I felt a rush of pride then, for this sweet little girl--so pretty and so well-behaved, she ought to be in movie--as if she were mine. I took a picture of her and the dog with my phone to send to Charlotte.

During the party I was supposed to watch a movie with Lily and put her to bed. To be honest, I was sad I was not invited, though it wouldn't make sense if I was. Sophie, however, was invited, which meant she couldn't go out with her friends. It was amazing to me--despite her sulkiness, she had acquired a whole posse of American girls, all as pretty and terrifying as she was. It's like they had some sort of whale call by which they greeted one another. This meant she was sulking all week, until Henry brought home a new dress for her; blue silk with embroidered sleeves, probably worth a month of my pay.

My mother once said that there are two kinds of people in the world. It's not rich and poor, it's people who think about how much something costs before they buy it, and people who don't.

Kayla called me one night, except she calculated the time difference wrong. Everyone else in the apartment was already asleep, and I could not talk above a whisper, which made our conversation difficult and unsatisfying. She told me that she was trying to get a degree in teaching, which was probably a good idea for her. It might mean leaving the city, which might mean us not seeing each other again for a really long time. Maybe never.

Did it make me a bad friend that this didn't bother me? She sounded happy. I felt happy for her. I wanted good things to happen to her. But I didn't care if I saw her again or not, any more than I cared if I saw Gillian or Kathy or a dozen other people who had, at one time or another, been my friends. It was as if we had all agreed, right from the start, to someday forget each other. Or maybe it was just me. Maybe I was the only one who floated away so easily.

The thing was, I really missed you. I just didn't know if it was you, exactly, or just a you-shaped memory, the best parts of you tied together with string and stored somewhere at the back of my brain. Maybe I missed New York, but only the city as I knew it with you--God knows I hated it most of the time I lived there. Or maybe--and this is the most likely explanation--I needed to miss someone, while I was living in this city where I knew no one. If I didn't, I might fade away for good.

The party, by the way, was a disaster. Not that I witnessed much of it, but I did hear Charlotte vomiting in the bathroom, which was sad. In the morning when I helped her clean up broken glass and flower petals and gravy stains, she didn't say a word.

Charlotte asked me one day why I was taking time off from school. I didn't want to tell her the whole truth but I gave a pretty substantial version, I think.

I said that I was really unhappy and I couldn't tell if it was because of the school or because of New York or because of myself. I said that I needed time to figure that out, and I didn't want my parents to be paying all that money just for me to be miserable.

When she asked if I was planning on going back, I lied and said yes. I had no idea what I was planning. Just thinking about it made me sick.

She told me that she took time off school, too. During her freshman year at Williams she was seeing a senior boy.

"Not a very nice person," she said, "but not a lot of guys are when they're that age. They can get away with anything and they know it."

This guy - she didn't tell me his name - had a girlfriend, another senior. Over Thanksgiving he died in a car accident. The whole campus went into mourning. "He was very popular," she explained. "It was a real shock."

The worst part, though, was that he'd told her to keep him a secret all that time, and so Charlotte had to pretend she was sad in the same way everyone else was sad. She went to the memorial service held by the college but she wasn't invited to his funeral. Why would she be?

"It made me feel like I was going insane," she told me. "My friends thought I was crazy, that I was so miserable about the death of a guy that, as far as they knew, I had never spoken to. At first they thought I was just sensitive, but they got sick of me eventually."

"And you never told them?" I asked.

"Never told anyone, not until after I'd graduated. I didn't want his girlfriend to find out. I was afraid everyone would hate me."

"It wasn't your fault," I said, dully.

"No." Her voice was very even. "But no one is going to blame a dead, beautiful boy for a youthful indiscretion."

"I'm sorry," I said. "That's really terrible."

Of course, this story made me think of you – another beautiful boy, another guy who knows he can get away with anything. It made me miss and worry about you, but it also made me wonder how I'd talk about you, years from then. I wondered how I would tell this story almost as much as I wondered how it would end.

One Friday I picked up Lily from school and took her home, where Charlotte was waiting for us, sitting in the kitchen with her hair pulled back into a ponytail and a book about French colonialism upside-down on the table.

I learned that if Charlotte had her hair back it meant she had some sort of plan in mind, which could range from Thai food for dinner (nixed by Sophie, who was allergic, apparently, to coconut) to a family trip to Weimar (nixed by Henry, who said it hadn't been interesting since the 19th century).

On that day, however, her plan was to go to a giant bookstore in Mitte. According to Charlotte, it was quite famous. We took a taxi, and I was able to tell the driver where to go, and he understood me perfectly, which caused Charlotte to give me a high-five with her gloved little hand.

The store was huge--I'd never seen anything like it. Charlotte was searching for some specific French book, so while she looked for that I took Lily to the kid's section and we spent about an hour there. I tried to get Lily to pay attention to the books but she was more interested in the stuffed animals. I didn't blame her. They were all large and expensive, plush and pleasantly heavy, the kind I coveted as a kid.

Charlotte must have seen me eyeing a gorgeous

Florentine stationery set because she bought it for me just as we were leaving. She asked the woman at the cash register to wrap it, so that it would feel like more of a present, even though I was standing next to her when she bought it. I kept saying thank you, thank you, over and over again like a little kid. She smiled, glowing, serene in the store's warm light.

All evening I had this glowing feeling. It was not entirely unfamiliar to me. I think I felt similar after the first time you kissed me, when I got my driver's license, when I got my first college acceptance letter... and at some other points in my life, maybe during my childhood, but I couldn't remember. Basically, times when I felt accomplished, or lucky, or satisfied.

In the past it had been a dangerous feeling, because by definition it can only last so long. For instance: as soon as you kissed me, I wanted you to kiss me again. Though I doubted that I'd spend my whole life waiting for Charlotte's next gift or high-five or kind comment. I was just trying to sit with that feeling, the sweetness and the fragility of it, trying to figure out how I could make it last.

On Friday the Herzfelds had friends over for a late dinner, and after I put Lily to bed, Charlotte invited me to join them. It wasn't a party or anything, just another couple, a woman Charlotte works with and her husband, but it was still very elegant and I was pleased to be allowed to join. The guest's names were Sarah and Fred Lerner. Fred was very handsome. I usually would not picture a man named Fred as handsome, and something about the disconnect between his name and his face made him even more attractive.

Sarah was pretty in the way that Charlotte was pretty, in the way that I was beginning to believe all wealthy thirty-something women were pretty: that highly-groomed, slightly frail look. They had the same haircut, and the same sharp knees visible through perfect jeans. But they didn't seem to like each other much.

They barely spoke, except to interrupt or agree with their husbands, who were arguing about European politics, which I didn't know enough about to tell who was correct. My instinct was to side with Fred, who spoke in a very slow, clear voice, rather than Henry, who got a little breathless while quoting statistics.

I did not actually learn anything because I drank a lot of wine and was too distracted by how sad Charlotte looked and how handsome Fred was. Situations like that made me think it was really pointless for me to ever go back to school. I couldn't concentrate on anything the way I could pay attention to a human face. I wasn't really interested in being a nanny for the rest of my life, but I couldn't think of another career that allowed me to watch people that closely.

Still, I managed to stay just sober enough to pretend I wasn't drunk at all, which was tricky. So that was my accomplishment for the evening. Sarah asked me some obligatory where-are-you-from questions and Fred ignored me entirely, which made me like him even more.

By the end of the dinner I decided that I didn't like Henry at all, whether or not that was justified. He was perfectly nice to me and seemed like a decent father. But he acted perpetually fed up with Charlotte, as if she was some clingy girlfriend following him around, and not his wife. I knew it was weird for me to be so protective of this grown woman, but I felt like someone ought to be.

It's not that I didn't enjoy working for the Herzfelds, but I liked Berlin best when I was by myself. I think I loved Berlin the way you might love a person, passionately and tenderly, but still with the underlying certainty that you will someday get sick of each other.

I loved the big empty field near our apartment, protected by barbed wire and thorns like a princess in a storybook. I loved the Jewish Cemetery, magnificent in its sadness. I loved the yellow street lamps and the smell of onions and the pristine little churches. When I walked home at night I loved the lambent windows of all the little houses, the brief glimpses of their chandeliers and bookshelves and kitchen tables. How can I explain it? I thought it was homesickness but it wasn't. It was this strange, protective feeling, a desire to freeze the world in a photograph so that it could not be harmed.

I went to Platz der Luftbrucke, which is the U-Bahnhof at which Isabelle Adjani has her famous breakdown in *Possession*. We watched that movie together, ages ago. You and me and Josephine and a bunch of your other friends, crowded around your couch, or lounging on your floor.

You were very excited to watch the movie and irritated that so many of your friends had shown up stoned, as if that wasn't something you yourself were so wont to do.

As much as I watched the movie, I watched you watching it. You were very still, except for your fingers, which you tapped against your knees as if playing an invisible piano, especially during tense scenes. Hands can be unexpectedly erotic objects. Sometimes I used to see you tie your shoes or hold a pen, and I felt as if I'd walked in on you naked.

Josephine was impatient. She kept checking her phone, getting up to get beer, crossing and uncrossing her legs. Occasionally you glanced at her in irritation, and she ignored you. I took pleasure in this. It made me feel that I was far more qualified than she to be your girlfriend.

I loved that movie. I really did. I especially loved the scene in Platz der Luftbrucke. My sadness never exploded like that, but if it ever did, I could only hope it would be so beautiful.

After, I took the train back to Prenzlauer Berg and went to a currywurst restaurant. The only thing I enjoyed more than currywurst is watching other people eat currywurst. I don't think I had ever tasted a food that is more obviously flesh, and the way people consumed it – always with some mix of grim determination and true delight – was wonderful. My mother called me that night and I didn't pick up because I just didn't have the energy.

Early one Saturday morning, I walked into the bathroom without knocking first and found Sophie at the edge of the bathtub, slicing at her hipbones with a razor blade. She glared at me, and my first thought was of a wounded animal. My second was of the street kids who begged for change by the Eberswalder U-Banhof, of their feral, pleading faces.

Instinctively, I closed the door behind me. She put down the razor blade, and it made a soft, tinny sound against the porcelain tiles. I sat down on the bathmat.

"Don't tell," she said.

"I won't."

It hadn't even occurred to me to do so, though I guess that would be the normal, adult response. My immediate reaction was the same as it would have been if Sophie were one of my friends in high school or college. I was curious and sympathetic and slightly envious. This was the strange, instinctive way in which girls add to their shared supply of secrets.

"I don't do it a lot," she said, defensively.

"It's OK," I said. "I'm not going to tell."

We stared at one another for a moment. "Do you want to talk about it?" I asked, uncertainly.

"Not really," she said, but I stayed where I was. Eventually she said, "Kind of. I do and I don't."

"How does it make you feel?"

"You sound like a shrink."

"I know." I was embarrassed. I realized I hadn't told Dr. Gordon I was leaving New York and she had never contacted me. For all that she knew, I could have jumped off a bridge since our last appointment. Her disinterest stung, but mostly I just felt like an idiot for caring.

"Have you ever done it?" Sophie asked, her voice sweet and quiet, like she was asking about my first kiss.

"A long time ago," I said.

"How did you stop?"

"I didn't need to anymore," I lied.

In truth, I stopped because I felt that I was getting too old for it, that it wasn't cute any more. Not that it ever was. But when you're sixteen, seventeen, there's a certain appeal to being a Sad Girl, a Fucked-Up Girl. There are plenty of guys that are into that.

That was my main seduction strategy, back when seducing people was something I enjoyed. I am so physically small and emotionally unstable that even the skinniest of hipster boys feel like Achilles in comparison.

I got tired of them, especially after I met you. I could no longer let those pretentious morons fumble around inside of me, no matter how easily I left my body, watching the whole sorry scene from the corner of the room.

But I was still cutting when I first met you. Only when I was drunk, though, and not because I was upset, but because it felt good. I loved the precision of the pain. Sometime shortly after I dropped out, I gave up on being a Sad Girl and got used to being a Sick Girl instead.

I helped Sophie disinfect the cuts and put on Band-Aids. I told her the story you told me, about a girl from your boarding school who went blind because she cut herself with a dirty knife and got an infection. Sophie pulled her skirt back down and stood up gingerly. "Don't tell," she said again, and I nodded.

Cutting had felt decadent. The day after I decided I wasn't going back to school, I treated myself to a box of razor blades in bright pink plastic cartridges, cotton swabs and rubbing alcohol.

To watch the blood bubble and seep from my skin was far more entertaining than any action movie or soap opera. I lay there on the floor of my old apartment, mesmerized for almost an hour, feeling lightheaded and warm.

Blood is its own metaphor. It speaks for itself.

In the living room, my roommates were smoking weed

and watching Spy Kids. I wondered what they would say if they knew: Oh, no, you should have told us you were feeling that way, we could have helped you, stopped you. But I didn't want any of that.

That was my only real addiction. Stranger than drugs, more tender than sex. And I could do it—I could only do it—on my own.

The first time we had sex, I wanted you to notice my scars, to comment on them. They're not that bad. Mostly they just make my legs look permanently dirty. But it disappointed me that you didn't say anything, until the third or fourth time, when you asked why, and I said I didn't know, I couldn't really remember.

"It made sense at the time," I told you, and you didn't ask again.

I finally called my mom, because it had been long enough that she might be reasonably afraid that I was dead. I tried to call when she'd be at work so I could just leave a message, but she picked up and I felt my heart sink. I knew I was a bad daughter. I just didn't feel like explaining my life to her. It exhausted me. I got stuck in this weird loop of irritation and guilt and by the end of our five-minute conversation I wanted to take a nap, but I had to go pick up Lily from school.

Lily seemed tired and quiet when I picked her up, which worried me a bit. I offered to stop and get her ice cream, and she just said, "it's too cold for ice cream." Which was true, but kind of a strange judgment call for a five-year-old to make.

When we got home, Sophie was watching television and doing her math homework. Usually she got home from school later in the evening because of tennis or whatever sport she played. Every time I saw her she was breathless and red-cheeked. On that day she was pale and withdrawn. I was dying to know why – boy problems? A bad grade? – but it would have been weird for me to ask and I doubted she'd answer truthfully. I made dinner (roast chicken with lots of rosemary, because I was feeling bored and ambitious) and we ate in silence.

That night Henry and Charlotte went to the opera with the Lerners and got back very late. The girls were asleep and I pretended to be, as well. Henry and Charlotte were in the kitchen, laughing and speaking softly. No matter how hard I tried, I could not make out their conversation.

The Lerners had a party to celebrate Sarah's fortieth birthday. It was on a Thursday night, which was usually my night off, but the Herzfelds paid me extra to stay and watch Lily. This was kind of perfect. I didn't have a lot to do on my nights off - mostly I went to watch movies by myself, which was fun, but not such a thrilling activity that I couldn't bear to miss it.

Charlotte was very excited and brought me (and Lily, by necessity) along to find something to wear. We started off with the stores near our apartment, which were all very hip, but Charlotte got impatient. Too much black, she said. Too many zippers. We took a taxi to KaDeWe.

While a painfully thin salesgirl helped Charlotte, I sat on a leather sofa with Lily on my lap. The weight of her was very comforting.

To keep her from getting bored I let her play a game on my cell phone. I tried to remember what I liked to do when I was five but it was a big blank. I couldn't read yet and my parents didn't let me watch television. Maybe I played with dolls. I don't know.

Lily was well behaved except when she got hungry or tired, which happened all of a sudden. She'd be fine and then ten seconds later she'd be crying. It was so hard to predict, but it was very easy to fix. The moment she started to wail, I picked her up in my arms and took her to the food court, where I got her a semi-baguette with cheese. The food court in KaDeWe was amazing, not just because all the food was gorgeous but because it was so quiet. There's nothing like that anywhere in America, I'm pretty sure. Quiet in a way that wasn't creepy, just peaceful and nice, like a church, or a museum, except everyone was eating, so it was more cheerful.

We wandered around there for a while, and I was considering spending the last of my pay from the previous week on a bouquet of marzipan roses, because I didn't know those even existed, but I realized I would just eat them all on my own, which would be kind of depressing. I would have stayed there longer but I wanted to see what Charlotte had chosen.

She was still in the fitting room when we got back, hands on hips, swaying slightly with a serious, stricken expression on her face.

"What do you think?" she asked me. She was wearing a black dress with lace at the hem, which ended right above her knee. The zipper was undone and I could see all the notches of her spine. She'd lost a lot of weight since we got to Germany.

"I thought you didn't want to wear black," I said.

"Everyone wears black, though, don't they? Especially here."

I shrugged. "So?" It was true everyone in Berlin wore

black, even more so than in New York. I thought it was boring, and worse, it reminded me of you.

"What do you think I should wear?"

I pointed toward a dress hanging on the door, made of yellow chiffon. "Something like that," I said. "Something kind of summery."

"It's fall!"

"Exactly. It'll cheer everyone up."

She seemed to like that idea. The salesgirl did not seem very happy with me. I found dresses in pale pinks and blues and greens, anything that reminded me of spring. "I'm too old to wear pink," Charlotte said, but she tried it on anyway.

"You look like a blonde Audrey Hepburn," I told her. Isn't that what everyone wants to look like? The woman too beautiful to be a sex symbol? But she actually did resemble her, a bit.

"Too old," she said again, and tried on a blue one.

"Like an Easter egg," she said. This went on for a while and I could tell she was getting depressed and Lily was getting sleepy.

I felt panicky. I looked to the salesgirl, who just stood with her arms crossed, scowling. Eventually I found a dress in the palest lilac, almost gray, made from silk so delicate I was afraid that if I touched it, it might dissolve.

The salesgirl seemed afraid of that, too. She took the

dress from me in a single swift motion and presented it to Charlotte, who finally grinned. That's the dress she bought, and I felt oddly proud of myself. It looked so good on her.

In New York I was always tired. In Berlin I was always hungry. I was allowed to eat out of the Herzfeld's fridge of course but I felt weird and self-conscious about it so mostly I ate street food. Enormous croissants for breakfast, currywurst and döners during the day, falafel late at night when nothing else was open. I knew I was getting fat – or fatter, at least – but I felt the excess flesh as a kind of comfort, like having a second self wrapped around me.

Certainly people – men, I mean, of course I mean men – didn't pay as much attention to me as they did in New York, and I missed it a little, especially when I was with Sophie, who was given free slices of cake almost every time we went to a café. (Always, always cake. Maybe that was just a Berlin thing.) Of course, I was the one who ate it.

Halloween made me think, painfully, of you, because it was the one holiday you genuinely cared about, even if it was as an excuse to corral people into watching horror movies with you. Interestingly, horror movies were one of the few things you had never been a snob about. You'd watch anything if a girl got cut into pieces at some point. We talked about this last year, when you convinced me to watch Suspiria with you. It's a real testament to how much I loved you because I hated that fucking movie. I hate all horror movies. I told you so afterwards.

You said, "It's because you identify with the victims, don't you?" And I said maybe it was true.

You were silent for a long time, then you said, "I identify with the killers, because that's how the movie's made. Made for men, at least. So for me it's kind of cathartic, and for you it's just your normal fears, amplified on a screen." You said this so tenderly that it took me by surprise. I'd half-expected you to make fun of me.

There were so many conversations like that, of which I could remember every single word, the inflection of your voice, the expression on your face, the points at which you coughed or laughed or sighed. For whatever reason, they got so stuck in my head. And yet I didn't know if you even remembered saying these things at all.

Early in November I got a very weird call around 5 p.m. It was my day off, and I had finally made it to Museum Island. Unfortunately, I had just finished walking around the Deutsches Historisches Museum, which was probably the most boring museum in Berlin, and perhaps the entire world (unless you are really, really into the fall of the Prussian empire, which I supposed someone must be) when the secretary from Lily's school called to ask if I could pick her up. I understood what she was saying but I answered in English, because I didn't know how to say, "Wait, did something happen?" in German.

"You tell me," she answered, sounding irritable.

"Where is Charlotte?" I asked.

"I don't know. We have been calling her. School ended an hour and a half ago. All the other children are gone. Do you know where Lily's mother is?"

"No. I don't. It's my day off."

"Well, you need to come get her. Everyone needs to go home."

"I'll be there as soon as I can."

I found Lily in the principal's office. Her face was splotchy from crying but she seemed relatively calm as she worked diligently on a coloring book. I picked her up and held her in my arms.

"What a big mistake Mommy and I made!" I said to her, and tried to wink at the secretary in order to indicate that I had it covered, but she merely stared impassively.

I got a cab to take us back to the apartment, even though it was walking distance, because I didn't want to put Lily down and I didn't think I could carry her all the way.

When we got back Sophie was doing her math homework in front of the television, which I was probably supposed to disapprove of, but I decided to get started on dinner instead. The three of us ate spaghetti with microwaved meatballs on the coffee table while Sophie's television show of choice, which was some sort of crime drama, played softly in the background.

I didn't think the show was really appropriate for Lily but it's sometimes confusing with kids – are they too young to register that something is violent, disturbing, wrong, or are they just old enough to be traumatized by it?

Feeling Lily had probably risked enough long-term psychological damage for one day, I asked Sophie to switch the channel, which she did reluctantly. We watched soccer until we finished eating.

"Thanks," I said to Sophie, as I washed the dishes. "Anyway, you know that the husband did it." She laughed, and I was relieved.

Charlotte woke me up one morning by calling for me from the other side of the apartment. She was in her bedroom, naked from the waist up, fiddling with a pair of earrings. She was so thin. In clothes she looked elegant, but without them she just looked ill.

When I saw her my body felt heavy and warm and unbearable, as if wearing a winter coat in summer. I know I said that my newfound flesh made me feel safe but in that moment it made me sick, like it was something strapped onto my body, like someone had played a mean trick on me.

"Have you seen my tall boots?" she asked. "I think I'm going to wear them today. I have a big meeting."

"I haven't seen them." I had never seen her wear tall boots, not that I could remember, and I usually paid a lot of attention to that sort of thing.

"Do you like this dress?"

"It's a nice dress. Is everything OK?"

"I'm nervous," she said. "It's a very big meeting."

"Why don't you sit down?"

She sat on the edge of her bed while I got her a glass of water, which she drank greedily.

"Are you hungry?" I asked.

"Not really."

"Do you want me to leave you alone?"

"Stay a moment." She patted the bed next to her. I

pretended not to notice.

"What are all those for?" I asked, gesturing to the neat line of orange bottles on her bedside table. Some of the names on the labels I recognized, others I didn't. I'd wanted to ask since she first showed me around the apartment, but this was the first time it felt even remotely appropriate.

"Happy, sane, calm, sleepy, focused," she answered. "Like Snow White and the Seven Dwarves."

I laughed.

"I hate the color orange," she said. "I tried keeping them in little ceramic pillboxes—I had all these pretty ones from my grandmother—but I got them all mixed up. I kept taking sleeping pills at eight in the morning. Not good."

"No, not good," I said, and thought of the time you forgot to get your Wellbutrin filled on time, of the scary, glazed way you moved around the world, of your hollow laughter.

I woke around dawn, and, unable to sleep, wrote you an email.

There was a time when I could always tell the second you walked into a room. Even if it was a party full of people, I'd know, right away. I could recognize you by your shadow. I could recognize you by your sigh.

I used to go to so many parties, because I wanted to be a person who was Good At Parties. I thought that was a real skill. I thought I would learn how to network or something. Like if the people at one party liked me enough, they'd invite me to another party, a better party, with better people, one of whom would eventually offer me a job, or marry me.

The other reason was that I always hoped to run into you, and I often did. It was for you that I washed my hair, for you that I wore miniskirts in December.

I did not press send, but I did not delete it, either.

I got paid extra to babysit all the kids at a Christmas Party in a big house on the outskirts of the city. There were six of them, most around Lily's age, peacefully playing video games, while I sat on a beanbag and tried to write you a letter.

Sophie was supposed to come but wanted to go out with her friends instead— a point of contention with Charlotte, who insisted that it was important the whole family be together for Christmas Eve. Sophie just stared at her for a while, with a disgusted expression that I translated as both *who gives a shit* and *what family*? She then asked Henry's permission, which he gave too easily, I thought, because Sophie seemed surprised by his answer.

I figured that she did in fact want to come along to this party, but she also wanted her father to insist that she did. Sometimes I felt like I saw all of them so clearly, and they saw each other so poorly, that I ought to step in, offer guidance.

But that's not what I was paid to do, and for all I knew, I was misreading everything, and they were a perfectly functional happy family and I was just looking for flaws because that's what I'm like.

Still, that evening was chaotic. We were late because Henry was yelling at Charlotte, half in English and half in German, which I thought was really cruel, because when Charlotte yelled back, "I don't understand!" she meant it

116

literally.

But German was Henry's first language, so maybe he wasn't trying to be cruel? I often gave men the benefit of the doubt, because if I didn't the only logical conclusion would be that they were all monsters.

You're all monsters? You never got offended when I said terrible things about men, partially because you could probably tell that it comes from a place of inchoate rage, and partially because I don't think you considered yourself a man. I'm not sure if I did, either. Maybe just because I liked you, and wanted to believe that you were somehow fundamentally different, or maybe because the delicate way you moved through the world confuses me, even now.

I think I liked working for the Herzfelds for the same reason you liked watching horror movies. It was both terrible and immensely satisfying to watch a beautiful thing rot from the inside out.

One Thursday, Henry came into the apartment in the middle of the day. We were surprised to see each other. I almost screamed but managed, thank God, to stop myself.

It was my day off, and I slept late because I had been up until dawn with Lily, who was having nightmares. Usually I was out of the apartment on Thursdays, wandering around the city. For all I knew, Henry always came home in the afternoons. For someone I lived with and worked for, I knew basically nothing about him.

But that day I was on the couch, sprawled out in a way I wouldn't have been if I knew someone might see me, watching *Taxi Driver* for the first time since high school. Cybil Shepard reminded me a lot of Charlotte in that movie: pretty in a goofy, vulnerable way. I paused the movie right as Robert de Niro was complaining that the smell of flowers made him sick.

Henry seemed out of it, maybe hung-over, maybe just tired, in a way that unsettled me, that made me wish I wasn't still in my pajamas. He looked at me like he couldn't remember who I was, and said hello very uncertainly.

"Hi," I said, feeling like I'd done something wrong, like I'd been caught breaking into the apartment. I felt like I ought to defend myself: I've lived here for three months!

"How are you?" he said, walking into the kitchen, pouring himself a glass of water.

"I'm fine. How are you?"

"Good. Good." He drank the water so quickly it made a sound as he swallowed, his throat rippling. I could see a few dots of blood on the underside of his jaw, where he must have cut himself shaving. "It's your day off?"

"Yeah." I felt defensive. "Every Thursday."

"Huh," he said, thoughtfully, like this was a piece of very interesting and original information, which he must take time to absorb properly. We were silent for a few minutes while he finished his glass of water.

I was acutely aware of my pajamas, of how inadequately they covered my shoulders and my knees, but I felt more ridiculous than obscene. Henry belonged to a category of men who I don't know well at all, but of whose existence I have always been acutely aware. Smart, wealthy men, who golf or ski or whatever. But it's less about money than this blissful, irritating confidence. No one has ever humiliated them.

When he went to put his glass in the dishwasher I got up and walked very quickly to my room. Then I sat there and waited for him to leave. It made me feel like a child, hiding under the covers: if I can't see the monster, he can't see me. When I heard the front door close behind him, I realized my face hurt from clenching my teeth.

In February, Peter came to Berlin for a few days. Kayla must have given him my new phone number. My instinct was to ignore him, but I guess I missed New York more than I thought, because I actually really wanted to see him.

I asked Charlotte if I could have Friday night off and she said that was fine. She seemed a bit better around that time, more with it. She and Sophie were even getting along, kind of.

Peter told me he was staying at The Circus Hotel, and I said I knew a good bar around there, which was not actually true. I just picked the first one that looked cool. A bar is a bar.

It wasn't too loud, so we sat in a corner with our beers and I listened to him talk about the project he was doing, some kind of video essay about his family's history, which sounded interesting, except that I had no doubt it would turn into some sort of aggressively artsy mess by the time he was done with it. I didn't really like Peter.

Partially it was irrational, because of my jealousy over his closeness with you, and partially I just thought he was an asshole. But I nodded along, asked a few questions, feigned reasonable enthusiasm. I was waiting, of course, for the conversation to turn toward you.

"Are you going to the wedding?" he asked me.

"I wasn't invited."

He raised his eyebrows.

"Maybe your invitation is late. International mail, you know."

"Maybe."

"Why do you think they're doing it?" he asked me.

"Getting married?"

"Yeah. Is she pregnant?"

"I wouldn't know. Maybe. Ask him."

To tell the truth, your engagement hurt me so much that it was hard for me to think of it as anything other than a kind of cosmic bullying. That there might be a totally normal, adult motive actually did not occur to me until then.

"I did ask. He got weird about it. Weirder than usual." He laughed, and I laughed too, like we were in on the same joke, which we weren't. He was laughing at you, and I was laughing because I knew that he and I were going to have sex, which was pretty funny to me. Peter, of all people, after all this time.

"Do you talk to him often?" I asked.

"No. Do you?"

"Occasionally."

"Do you miss him?" I asked. He looked at me like I was an idiot.

"No. He's boring whenever he's dating anyone and a million times worse engaged. When he gets married I fully expect him to slip into a fucking coma."

This I laughed at, genuinely.

Maybe that was one of the benefits of keeping everything a secret— I never had to deal with your other self, the boring one. I never even realized he existed. It made me feel sorry for Josephine, which made me feel superior to her, which made me feel happier than I'd felt in a long time. I paid for my drink and asked Peter if he wanted to go for a walk.

He did, and we walked for a while, stopping outside of a jazz club to listen to the music for a little while. The sound quality was surprisingly good. Peter leaned against the building, checking his cell phone. He seemed bored, which made me anxious.

"Let's keep going," I said, and sure enough, we ended up back at his hotel. It was that easy. I knew that it would be.

After, I went into the bathroom, turned on the faucet, lay down on the floor and cried for what might have been five minutes but felt like an hour. I was so hollow.

I wanted to pretend sex was like any other distraction available to me, that I could just as easily have gotten drunk or stolen some of Charlotte's valium. I wanted to pretend there was some value to the dull pain between my legs, that it reminded me I existed, that I had a body that belonged entirely to me, that it was not just the same discomfort I'd experienced a million times.

I could tell that I was spiraling, allowing one bad thought to cling to another until they formed a kind of whirlpool in my head, punctuated occasionally, of course, by your face. I cried like a child, and cried more because I felt like a child, and because no one except for Peter even knew where I was.

Eventually I tired myself out. I washed my face and braided my hair and went back into the bedroom. If, in the half-light, Peter could tell that I'd been crying, he said nothing.

It was two in the morning— not too late for me to get dressed and go home, but I was tired and stubborn and empty, and so I climbed back into bed with him, and he let me curl up next to him, resting my head on his bony shoulder.

He was so tall— even taller than you, I noticed—and

next to him I felt wonderfully small. This soothed me, as did Peter's quiet breathing, and the faint sound of techno music playing downstairs. I fell asleep, not happy, exactly, but more calm than I'd been in a long time.

I woke up too early. Peter had not closed the blinds, and the room was flooded with cold, clean light. I laid on my back with my hands pressed against my stomach, trying to keep it from rumbling. Though I could have left and bought myself breakfast quite easily, I wanted to wait until Peter woke. I wanted to say goodbye, at least.

It is a horrible lonely feeling, to wake up next to someone who does not love you, to watch them sleep and feel absolutely certain that they are dreaming about someone else. I was disappointed by how sentimental I was getting about the whole thing. And with Peter, of all people. I imagined Kayla laughing at me. With me, maybe.

After an hour or so the hunger became unbearable and I started to get dressed. Peter woke as I was pulling on my tights. He smiled, beautifully, his eyes not quite open. It reminded me of you, and made my lungs heavy with sadness. Everyone knows men are vulnerable to beauty. You see it in every movie, read it in every poem. I did not know that I was capable of that same weakness.

I left my sweater in Peter's room. I left it in a very obvious place, right on his desk, so that he would have to be a real asshole not to try to return it. But he was, and so he didn't, and I regretted it because it was a nice sweater: black, made of real cashmere, from a secondhand store near the Eberswaldestrasse store. It had been worn just the right amount to make it exquisitely soft.

When I was in high school I stole things. Not a very original form of rebellion, I know, and it didn't last long. A lot of girls like the thrill of it, the giddy fear of getting caught, but what I liked was the objects themselves. I only stole little things. Earrings, lipsticks, paper weights, small animals made of glass. I liked things I could keep in my pocket, tangible secrets. But I hated that scared feeling, and I guess the fear won out.

Years later, I started to do what I guess is kind of the opposite, which is leaving things in other people's homes, to see how they'll react. I must have sacrificed half a dozen hair clips, as many earrings, a couple pairs of tights, and at least one really nice bra in this way. Freshman year, I left my copy of Augustine's Confessions in the office of a professor I had a crush on, with my name and cell phone number written on the inside cover. He returned it via campus mail and avoided eye contact with me for the rest of the semester.

Morally, this was probably a better practice, but it was

even more dishonest. Stealing, at least, was an obvious act. You take something because you want it. What I did was more sinister because no one, least of all me, really knew why I was doing it.

My mother's sister Danielle died in March. My father called to tell me. Heart failure, age forty-five. Danielle had, for a long time, been the black sheep of the family, a tornado of a woman. The last time I saw her, when I was still in high school, she'd been out of rehab for two weeks, and was asking my parents to loan her money to set up her own jewelry company. I remembered she gave me "sample pieces" -- delicate silver bracelets that didn't fit around my wrists, and crystal earrings so heavy it hurt to wear them.

I didn't like being in the same room as her. Her voice was unnerving, high and whiney like a child's, but raspy from decades of smoking. She smelled too strongly of lavender. I remember her wearing the same black cocktail dress nearly every day, its shiny fabric riding up when she sat down. She frightened me.

My father hated her. He didn't even bother to disguise it. Eventually my mother agreed to stop inviting her to stay, deciding that she was a bad influence on me. Actually, I think it was the opposite. Danielle gave me a very clear picture of what I didn't want to be.

Charlotte, of course, allowed me to go home for the funeral. She was very kind and sympathetic.

"Were you two close?" she asked.

"Not really," I said. "But I want to be there for my mom."

"Of course. Of course."

At the airport I sent you an email. I didn't expect you to reply but it felt good to write it.

Do you remember a picture like this: a photograph of a woman standing on a chair, wearing high heels. A man's hands are wrapped around her ankles. I think you showed it to me, in a book. Or in the pages of a magazine, or in a subway ad. I don't know. But it haunts me. If you know what I'm talking about, will you tell me?

On the plane home I took several sleeping pills but they just made me nauseous. I thought about Danielle, trying to figure out what the turning point in her life was, the moment at which she went from a garden-variety party girl to full-fledged addict, and if it had something to do with the terrible boyfriends my parents whispered about, or the ex-husband I never met. I wondered if it was sudden or gradual. I was not as judgmental of her as I had been when I was younger, probably because it was very easy to imagine myself turning out the same way.

I did have a couple good memories of her. When I was six or seven my mother and I visited her in Boston. Danielle's apartment was too small so all three of us stayed in a hotel. I remember sitting in bed and watching television with Danielle while my mother was out shopping. Danielle was smoking, and occasionally leaned over and covered my eyes with her hand if there was something inappropriate on the screen. She had long nails painted red, and to me she seemed impossibly glamorous. The smell of cigarettes still made me nostalgic.

My mother picked me up from the train station in Amherst and we went to lunch together. As I probably told you, my parents tended to drive me kind of insane, mostly because they are so infuriatingly normal. Like every child, I fantasized that they were not my real family, that I was the daughter of artists or monarchs or movie stars, who would come to retrieve me sooner or later. However, since none of my relatives have red hair, I managed to sustain this fantasy a little bit longer than I guess is strictly normal. It wasn't until puberty, when I inherited my mother's small, sturdy body and large breasts, that I accepted my genetic fate.

I was embarrassed of my parents, and I was ashamed of my embarrassment, because after all they were paying for my psychiatrist, and some of my rent, and my education, or at least what existed of it. So I knew I had no right to feel such contempt, but I did, I did.

My bedroom was the same as I left it, so pink and blue and pristine. I felt like such an intruder, like someone who snuck into a museum after hours, someone who was about to ruin something good.

My dad was a dermatologist and my mother taught French at a private Catholic boys' school. They were the kind of people that, for you, did not really exist. I think your world was made up entirely of artists and millionaires. Didn't Josephine's parents work in television? I think Kayla told me that.

Still, they were not totally insensitive to the things we loved. My dad, for instance, could recite a lot of Wilfred Owen, for some reason. My mother assigned her more advanced students *No Exit* and *The Stranger.* I think at some point they liked the idea of having an artistic daughter, an intellectual daughter, or whatever, but by some point they changed their mind and just wanted a kid who was normal.

I hated it when they touched me. I flinched whenever my mother hugged me or tucked my hair behind my ear. She was hurt, and I was frustrated, because of course she was upset, but how could I control something like flinching?

The weird thing was that I didn't mind it when strangers touched me. In fact, I often loved it. There was a period of time during which I kept donating blood because I liked the tender way the Red Cross people touched the inside of my elbow, a part of my body, I felt, that didn't get touched nearly enough. At parties I kissed boys I'd never met before with such abandon that Kayla once remarked

132

that I made out with everyone like I was in love.

All the clothes I owned that were appropriate for a funeral fit too tightly then, so I had to borrow a dress of my mother's, a pale gray shift that made me look somewhat like a whale. A petty concern given the circumstances, I know, but one that irked me anyway.

There were all of thirty people there, most of them my mother's friends, who had never met Danielle but came to support her. I got a lot of tentative hugs from people I vaguely recognized.

The rabbi greeted me with a firm handshake and a sorrowful expression. I wondered how many people he'd given that same solemn look. I couldn't remember the last time I was in a real synagogue. When I was a kid we went to Yom Kippur services in the basement of a local high school, and that was only when we really felt like it.

The whole thing seemed so forced. Danielle would have hated every aspect of this, I thought, and for the first time since my father told me she was dead I felt something like a punch to my throat.

My mother gave a short speech. Even with the help of a microphone, her voice was barely audible. She told a story about how when they were children, Danielle wanted a cat so badly that she pretended to be one, meowing and crawling around on all fours, until their parents gave in and bought one. Everyone laughed politely. I'd heard this story before, and liked it, but in this context it seemed less funny and more apocryphal.

Over the phone, my father had asked me to write something I could read.

"Just a short poem or something," he said. "It would mean a lot to your mother." It wasn't an unreasonable request—what's the point of studying literature if you can't even come up with a decent elegy?—but I couldn't, and so instead I read Rilke's "Lament," from the book you gave me for my birthday last year. I carried it with me to Berlin and back. The sight of my name in your hand on the inside cover tugged at me, and I was crying too hard to finish reading.

I sat down next to my mother, and she held me, and we both cried, her mascara leaking onto my shoulder, leaving a stain. That I was not crying for Danielle— not totally, at least — made me feel guilty, but I think she of all people might have understood.

On the plane to Berlin I sat next to a woman with short dark hair who took several pills and swallowed them without water before we took off. We exchanged the bare minimum of pleasantries before she started reading a German-language fashion magazine and I began to watch a fairly generic action film. Halfway through the movie I fell asleep and dreamed about buildings turned inside out and guns glued to my hands.

The woman next to me slept so deeply that when we landed I had to nudge her awake. She smiled apologetically, the magazine open upside-down on her lap. As I watched her struggle to get her suitcase out of the overhead compartment, I thought that if I was a man, that's the type of woman I would try to seduce. The ones with airplane sized bottles of Jack Daniels in their purses, nails they painted themselves, knee length skirts. The ones who think no one can tell they're wearing last night's eyeliner. The ones who think it's still an adventure.

(When did I start thinking like this? How did my heart get so ugly?)

Charlotte promised to pick me up at the airport. I even e-mailed her my flight information the day before. But after half an hour of waiting, watching the tourists and businessmen and security guards swirling around me, I realized something must have come up.

In the taxi I thought of you, and I realized I was running out of ideas about you. There are only so many memories you can get out of a year. I found myself wishing I had worked harder to spend time with you, as if I could have done so without surgically attaching myself to your body. I began to worry that I was going to run out of things to say about you, long before I ran out of love for you.

When I got to the apartment, I could hear music playing from Charlotte and Henry's room, something jazzy and calm. I thought Charlotte might be doing yoga. I knocked on the door and then opened it without waiting for a reply.

In the clean morning light, Charlotte was lying face-down on her bed and Fred was fucking her from behind. The idiotic, pained look on his face made me think of the boys I knew in elementary school, the ones who spent recess stepping on ants and throwing rocks at squirrels, before they found out that girls made more interesting prey.

Charlotte was flat on her stomach, head turned to the side, her legs splayed out at terrible angles. She reminded me of a ragdoll or a mannequin, something that could not feel pain, only absorb it. She lifted her head slightly when I walked into the room, but her face did not change. How many times had I worn that exact same face, the half- drugged mask of a body that has decided to rid itself of a brain?

I could not stand to be in the room for more than three seconds. I went into the bathroom and vomited into the sink, a combination of airplane food and funeral hors d'oeuvres and a little bit of blood. It was a strangely satisfying experience. It made me feel both in control of my body and blissfully removed from it, as if I were a robot functioning exactly as I ought to.

I lay on the floor for maybe a minute before realizing that I was sick of lying on bathroom floors and instead decided to clean the sink. Then I washed my face, brushed my teeth, and put on my coat.

Once I was out of the apartment, I looked down the stairs and thought, dreamily, of falling. It was you who once told me that Zelda Fitzgerald threw herself down a marble staircase because her husband flirted with someone else at a party. "My kind of girl, Zelda," was what you said, and it made me happy, because I thought maybe I fit into that category, and that I was, by extension, your kind of girl.

But I took one step, and then another, and then got distracted by the thin blades of light against the white walls, and before I knew it I was at the bottom and out the door.

I took the tram to Mitte and found Peter's hotel. In German, I asked the receptionist if he was still staying with them. She replied in English that he had left that morning for Prague.

I asked if she had a forwarding address or a telephone number. She looked at me skeptically. Her eyes were very blue and she had a small crucifix tattooed in the crook of her elbow.

"I have some important news to give him," I said.

She considered. I gave her my best I-am-not-insane look.

"Why don't you give me a message and I promise I will get it to him."

I nodded and she gave me a piece of paper with the hotel's tiny logo printed at the top. In my neatest handwriting I wrote: *Call me*, and then my number, and then drew a small, sloppy bird, hoping to add a little mystery to my missive. I thanked the concierge warmly and went back outside.

Propelled by emptiness, I walked all the way back to the apartment. Charlotte was in the kitchen, fiddling with an elaborate Japanese teapot I'd convinced her to buy. She was dressed in a long, fluffy robe that exposed her ankles. Her hair was wet.

"Hello," I said.

"Hello," she said. "Would you like some tea?"

Is this what we're doing? I wanted to ask. Is this really how we're going to proceed? I was disappointed. "Yes, please." I said.

"How was going home?"

"Fine," I said. "But it's nice to be back."

"I'm glad. I'm so glad. The girls are with Henry, visiting his parents."

"That's nice."

"Yes, it is. We should do something special, just the two of us."

"Like what?"

"Oh, I don't know. Get manicures. Buy shoes. Whatever you like." She laughed weakly.

"I think I'm going to read," I lied.

"That's nice," she said, smiling beatifically. I could have slapped her.

I really would have liked to read, actually, except that I couldn't think of a single book that would tell me exactly how I ought to feel. Instead I lay on the floor with my headphones on, listening to the kind of music you never liked, hoping for some clues in the high notes of women whose hearts were far more broken than my own.

The Wednesday after Henry and the girls returned home, I received a call from a number I did not recognize. I was trying to nap, and it woke me from the unpleasant state I was resting in, somewhere between boredom and a nightmare. A woman with an English accent said that she was calling from the American school, and before I could answer, put Sophie on the line.

"Hi?" she asked. Her voice sounded so small I barely recognized it.

"Hi Sophie. What's going on?" I sat up quickly, hitting my elbow on the headboard.

"I need you to come pick me up."

"Can't you just take a cab?"

"No, I need you to come pick me up." We were both silent for a few seconds. "I'm in trouble," she said.

My heart went still. "What kind of trouble?"

"Like, I got in trouble."

"Like a punishment?"

"Yeah." She sounded irritable.

"Oh. Like in trouble with your school?"

"Yes."

"I thought you meant like, you had been kidnapped, or something." "What?"

"Never mind." I felt excruciatingly silly as I pulled on my boots and coat. "I'll come get you now."

Sophie's school was in a pretty, tree-lined neighborhood.

It could have been Connecticut as easily as Berlin. Above me, the wind through the leaves made a single, shimmering sheet of green. It took some wandering to find the principal's office, where Sophie was seated primly with her back to the door, fiddling with her phone.

"You're not Mrs. Herzfeld, are you?" asked the principal, an elegant, weary woman with wispy blonde hair.

"I'm her assistant," I said. It was only sort of a lie.

"I was hoping she could be here herself," she answered. "I would like to speak with her directly."

"She's at work," I answered. "I apologize."

The woman looked at me skeptically and then gestured for me to sit down. Sophie did not meet my eyes.

"We found this in Miss Herzfeld's locker during a routine check," she said, pulling a small red Swiss Army knife from her desk. "As I'm sure you know, we have a zero tolerance policy for weapons on our campus."

"Yes, but that's not really a weapon, is it? I mean, you can use it to cut your nails," I said.

She glared. "Zero tolerance," she repeated.

"I see," I said. "Well, maybe it was just a misunderstanding."

"That's what I was hoping. But when I asked Miss Herzfeld why she had this item, she refused to answer, and demanded that I call her lawyer."

I had to suppress a laugh.

"As it is, I have no choice but to suspend her."

"Is that really necessary?" I asked. "Like I said, it's hardly a weapon. Obviously it was stupid of Sophie to bring it to school, but you don't really think she was planning to harm anyone, do you? Because if you do, then that's a very serious accusation, and in that case I think she's right, we should call our lawyer and have him sort this out."

"Zero tolerance," she said again, but more weakly.

"I understand completely. And I appreciate you being so thorough in regards to your students' safety." I wasn't sure where the words were coming from, but they seemed to be working. "But this was clearly just a matter of poor judgment. Perhaps Sophie can perform community service, or write a letter of apology, or something like that?"

The principal was silent for a minute.

"Four pages," she said, finally. "Single spaced. On the potential risks posed by bringing a weapon, even a minor one, to school. Due tomorrow morning. You're dismissed from classes from the rest of the day. Please take the rest of the day to think seriously about your actions."

Sophie, still mute, nodded. As she gathered her things I shook the principal's hand. She looked completely exhausted and I felt sorry for her.

We took the U-Bahn back to the apartment in silence. Not until we got inside did she ask, "Are you going to tell my dad?"

"Um. I probably should."

"Please don't. If I write the paper he won't even have to find out."

"Were you using the knife to cut yourself?"

"Yeah. Duh."

"That's not good, Sophie."

"I mean, at least I wasn't planning on like, stabbing anyone."

"I know, but still."

"Please. I'll stop."

"Cutting?"

"Yeah."

"It's not that easy."

"I'll see a therapist. I'll see the school counselor, at least. She's supposed to be really good. A lot of my friends say they like her."

I knew I was going to lose this argument. After all I didn't want to have that conversation with Henry any more than Sophie did.

"I want to read the essay before you turn it in," I said, even though I didn't. "OK. OK! That's fine." Her face was flushed with relief. I felt both benevolent and incompetent.

On the day of your wedding, Peter called me.

"I wanted to see if you were OK," he said. I was so surprised that I did not answer for a minute.

"Are you there?"

"Yes. Yes, I'm great."

"Good. OK, Bye."

"Wait!" I was, in fact, fine. I wouldn't have expected myself to be so calm, but I was. Still, I wanted to talk to him.

"Yeah?"

"How are you?" I asked.

"I'm OK."

"I mean, I know you're OK. Like, in general. Are you still in Prague?"

"Yeah."

"Is it nice there?"

"It's nice."

His voice was quiet and terse and I wondered if he was regretting whatever kind impulse prompted him to call me.

"And your project?"

"It's kind of a mess."

"Oh, that's too bad. It sounded cool." In truth, I could not really remember much about his project, except that he had gotten uncharacteristically breathless while talking about it.

146

"I could use help," he said, suddenly. "If you're ever in Prague. With like, archiving, and shit."

"I don't think I'm going to be in Prague any time soon," I said, stupidly. There was another long silence.

"But maybe," I added.

"Maybe," he repeated.

"It was really nice of you to call."

"Yeah, well. Take care."

"You too."

He hung up and I flopped onto my bed, feeling loose and warm.

I thought of Josephine. I imagined her as a young girl in a school uniform, as a college student staring adoringly at a professor. I imagined her at work, typing away furiously, her hair tied up in a sensible bun. I imagined her getting ready for the wedding, with hairdressers and make-up artists and female relatives swirling around her.

There was a time I couldn't imagine anything better than a team of people preparing me to marry you, beautifying me accordingly. Now it made me dizzy and sad. I felt a strange sense of comradeship. I thought I ought to start a support group for us, all the stupid girls who were in love with you.

I thought of Sarah, Fred's pretty wife, who had not crossed my mind since Christmas Eve. It occurred to me that we were all locked in a battle, the mistresses versus the wives. I was sick of it. If that was what being a woman was like, then I wanted out.

A couple days after the incident at school, I found Sophie in her bedroom, lying on the white carpet reading Heart of Darkness, or at least trying to. She had big, expensive headphones on, and I had to take them off her head in order to get her to notice me. When she did, she gave me a look like I was some kind of particularly irritating ghoul risen from the grave just to annoy her. I was a little offended.

"How are you?" I asked, primly.

"Great," she said.

"Sophie."

"What?"

"You know what." I heard my own mother's voice come out of my mouth and tried not to cringe. "I need to see your arms," I said, sternly.

"I don't cut my arms."

"Where do you cut?"

"My thighs." She gestured toward her legs, clad in tight jeans.

"Well, I'm not going to make you take your pants off," I said, uncertainly. "I need you to promise that you're not hurting yourself anymore."

"I promise."

"How's the counselor?"

"She's good."

"What's her name?"

"Hilde," she answered, exasperated. "She's Austrian. Super nice."

"What did you two talk about?"

"Doctor-patient confidentiality," she answered.

"Sophie."

"Look, if I tell you it defeats the whole entire purpose." She had a point.

"I'm trying to look out for you."

"I know you are." Her voice softened. "Thanks."

My heart felt large at that moment, and I was, paradoxically, so proud of the secret I was keeping that I wanted to show it off to everyone. Instead, I leaned down and gave Sophie a hug, which she returned, tentatively.

A week later, after I brought Lily home from school, I was surprised to find Henry waiting for us in the apartment. He was sitting on the living room sofa, fiddling with his cell phone. He barely looked up when we walked in.

"May I have a minute?" He asked. I nodded.

"Go wash your hands," I told Lily. "I'll be there in a minute."

I sat down across from him.

"Is everything alright?" I asked. It was a stupid question.

"I'm afraid Charlotte and I think it is time we let you go."

I did not respond, only sat staring back at him, feeling my heart freeze over.

"You've been a great help to us. You've been excellent with Lily. I'm very sorry. We will, of course, pay you through the end of the month, and compensate you for your plane ticket back to New York."

He looked at me expectantly. I studied his face, the skin around his jaw just beginning to sag, the lines around his eyes that made them look beady rather than bright. I could tell he used to be handsome. More handsome than Fred, even. I wondered if men missed their beauty the way that women did. I wished I could ask him.

"You've been a great help," he said again. "Unfortunately we have to let you go. I'm sure you understand why."

"Not really," I said, finally.

He sighed, sort of melodramatically, I thought.

"We got a call from Sophie's school. Regarding an incident last week."

"Oh."

"She said Charlotte's assistant had promised to pass along the message."

"Right. I forgot."

"You're not Charlotte's assistant."

"I kind of am," I said, defensively.

"Anyway. We can't have someone keeping things like that from us. It's inappropriate."

He said "inappropriate" the way someone else might say "repulsive" or "perverted." I felt tears building and wanted nothing more than to run out of the room, but I stayed in my place.

"We know you meant well," he continued. "But you work for us, not Sophie. She's still a child, you know. Maybe the two of you are too close in age, and it made things confusing. But it shows poor judgment on your part, and we no longer feel that you should work for our family. I am sure you understand."

"And what does Charlotte say about all this?"

"She says what I say," he answered, confused. "We don't think you should continue to work for us."

"OK. Yeah, sure." I felt a little sick, but not hopeless. Nothing Henry said sounded like Charlotte in the slightest. I felt sure that if I could just speak to her, we could work something out.

"I'll book you a flight for Friday. That will give you enough time, correct?" Henry started to stand up.

You won't survive a day without me, I thought.

"Correct."

"Alright. Please give Lily dinner. Charlotte should be back before seven. I will see you tomorrow." He spoke haltingly, as if English had become suddenly unfamiliar to him.

Why did you become a father? I wanted to ask. It didn't suit him at all. Did he just assume it was what you were supposed to do with your life? What the hell was he thinking?

I went into Lily's room. She was rearranging the furniture in her dollhouse, her little hands moving as carefully as a surgeon's. I picked her up in my arms and held her for a while. She buried her face in my shoulder. Children are never so stupid as to reject affection. They are much more intelligent than adults in this way.

Henry was wrong. Charlotte didn't return home until after nine. Lily was already in bed. Sophie was in her room with the door shut. She hadn't said a word to me. I wondered if she knew.

"Hi," I said, and Charlotte jumped a little.

"Hi! How are you?"

I stared at her for a moment.

"I'm fired," I said.

"Oh, sweetheart," she said, and hugged me. "You're not fired. We just think this isn't a good fit. That's all."

Her eyes were unfocused, smudged with mascara. Beneath her beautiful perfume, she smelled like she hadn't showered in days.

"Henry fired me," I said, slowly. "I am fired. I am going home."

"I know you must be upset. But I think it will be good for you to go home. To go back to school. Weren't you saying you wanted to go back to school?"

"No. I never said that. I don't want to go home."

"Well, maybe you can travel a bit. Have you been to Budapest? I think you would love Budapest. Or even Paris. Why don't you go to Paris?"

"Are you high? I can't just go to Paris." I could no longer contain my tears. It was humiliating, but Charlotte didn't seem to notice.

"Don't you want to see your family? Don't you miss

them?"

"Yes," I said, "but that's not the point."

"I think you would love Budapest," she said again.

Exhausted, I sat down on the couch. I thought of Peter's offer. Archiving and shit. Why shouldn't I go to Prague?

"I guess you're right," I said. She sat down next to me and stroked my hair. Her hands were cool and smelled of peppermint.

"It's for the best, really. You have to trust me. We're not just turning you out on to the street, I promise. We'll make sure you get where you want to go. I'll write you a letter of recommendation. This is the best thing for everyone."

I turned to her in sudden horror.

"It's your idea, isn't it? You want to get rid of me."

"Don't be silly," she said, but would not meet my eyes.

"Charlotte, I would never tell anyone, you don't have to worry –"

"I don't know what you're talking about." She stood up, a little wobbly. "You must be very upset," she said, quietly. "Why don't you have an early night. We can talk about this in the morning."

I was so full of rage that I had nothing else to say.

I did think very seriously about going to Prague. I imagined myself exploring the castle, wandering through museums, visiting Kafka's house, Peter by my side, a string of garnets glittering around my neck. I was particularly enchanted by a picture of the castle covered in snow, rising about a silver river. Was I really going to stay through the winter? Well—why not? It was a beautiful city, with a rich history, and I knew someone who lived there. I could probably find a job at a restaurant or a hotel. Czech couldn't be so much harder than German. If nothing else, I might get my sweater back. What was stopping me from going to Prague? What was stopping me from anything?

Except, that was more or less what I'd thought about Berlin. I thought the city could save me. I hoped I would disappear into museums and monuments, that I would emerge stronger and smarter and totally unrecognizable. And yet you had followed me there, pulling at my hair, whispering in my ear. Even worse, I had followed myself.

I called Kayla, but she didn't pick up. I wanted to leave a message but couldn't think of what to say. I wondered what New York might be like, now that I had lost you for good. I still couldn't tell where you ended and the city began. If someone asked me to draw a map, all the landmarks would be yours: this is where you first touched my arm, this where you kissed me for the last time, this is where I cried for you, this is where missing you made me wish I was dead, this is where I thought I saw you, and called out to you, but it was someone else entirely.

It might be good for you to go home, Charlotte had said. As if it were so easy to locate.

I was not a good daughter, and maybe that's why I tried so hard to be a good girlfriend. Given the opportunity, I would have tried to be a good wife, too. I might have even made an OK mother, if circumstances demanded it. Being a nanny was some combination of all those roles. I thought I was doing a decent job, even if recent events suggested otherwise. That's what felt so desperately unfair. I thought I was finally getting it right.

I imagined a huge playing field, brilliant green, marked with white lines. On one side were the wives and girlfriends of the world, the Sarahs and the Josephines, linking arms, marching forward. On the other were the mistresses, or whatever you wanted to call us, running around in circles, doing jumping jacks, tripping over each other's feet. From the sideline, men watched us, eating popcorn, only half paying attention. I wanted to call for a truce, or at least a time out. There had to be some other way to live.

Before I left, I went into Charlotte's room and found her jewelry box. Her bed was unmade and the whole room smelled of her - not just of her perfume but of Charlotte herself, her skin and her sweat and the peppermints she ate and the soap she used. It was so overwhelming that I had to sit on the bed with my head between my knees for a few minutes. I knew no one would be home for at least another hour, but I worked quickly. Charlotte's jewelry box was in her dresser, buried under a pile of sweaters. The box itself was made of red leather and shaped like a crescent moon. I took a string of tiny gray pearls. I closed the box and returned it to its hiding spot.

Once I had thought that by being on the edge of real lives—yours, Charlotte's— I would learn something vital about how to be a person. What a disappointment. You were all children playing dress up, running around in your grown up clothes. And I was still tugging at your shirtsleeves, begging for answers.

At the airport I spent the last of my cash on German chocolate, two bottles of Maker's Mark, and a set of miniature Dior perfumes. Presents for my parents, I decided. Maybe I'd give one of the perfume sets to Kayla, if she ever called me back. I thought of her enormous grin and felt a longing as pure as any I ever felt for you.

While I waited for my flight to board I read a magazine. Ten tips for better sex, twenty ways to get him to commit, five signs he's cheating, etc., etc. It made me exhausted to be a woman. Sitting across from me, a mother with messy dark hair was putting hand sanitizer on her two little children, who were yelling and wriggling around. She was shushing them and trying to hold them still, but she was giggling, too.

On the plane, I was seated between an exhausted businessman and a grumpy blonde woman in athletic gear. Neither of them spoke to me. I unzipped my backpack and took out *War & Peace*. I had lugged it all the way to Germany without opening it once, and now, I felt, was as good a time as any to read. Because I could not remember where I left off, I started at the beginning. The story felt both familiar and completely new. The woman with her two children were seated in the row across from me.

As the plane took off, one of the children began to wail. The woman took him out of his seat and held him in her arms. The other passengers glared at her, and then looked at each other, grimacing, shrugging their shoulders. In their annoyance, there was an odd sense of comradeship. The woman smiled at me, apologetically, and I smiled back, as if to say, don't worry about it.

I remember a quote from Simone Weil, which you scribbled on a bright blue post-it note and stuck to your fridge: *love is not consolation. It is light.*

Who, then, will console me?

I thought of one spring day in New York, when you met me after work and we took the subway back to your apartment. You rarely took public transportation, preferring to pay for a cab or else walk distances anyone else would consider absurd. But on that day you were goofy and distracted – happy to see me, maybe – and forgot both your wallet and your gloves at home. When I held onto the pole for balance, you wrapped your hand over mine. You were standing right behind me so that your arm was pressed against the back of my neck. Your hand was so much larger than mine that it covered it entirely. It was amazing to me, how easily you touched me, like it was something you had done your whole life.

I knew, even before the moment ended, that it was one I would remember for a long time. I was nostalgic for something that hadn't ended yet, and so I existed, for a while, within the pristine state of memory. And yet as I sat on the plane, trying to fall asleep, I recalled it as if it were a movie I'd watched without sound, something so vague and distant it seemed impossible that I had ever really been there at all.

As the plane began to touch down, my heart started to beat furiously, and I had an urge to grab the hand of one of the people sitting next to me. Instead I clasped my hands together, almost like I was praying, squeezing my fingers so tightly that the pain cleared my head.

There was a point when the idea of returning home, even for a short while, would have seemed like a failure, a retreat from my real life. Now I felt that nothing could be so easily categorized, that there was no winning, and no losing, either. There was only living, and no one was going to teach me how to do it.

I knew I was a little young to be making that kind of pronouncement. It occurred to me that if I was still in school I might have written an essay in which that was the thesis. Or else I would have said it to some long-haired, sleepy-eyed boy who was only pretending to pay attention. As it was, I had nothing to do but recite it to myself, staring out the window as the city grew larger, the lights almost unbearably brilliant.

Who can sustain an escape from one's self? I wanted to ask you that. Was getting married enough? Once, I'd been so afraid you would forget me. Now I knew you wouldn't, but it didn't make me feel any better. You can't live inside of a memory, any more than you can live inside of someone else's life. I felt the strings that tied me to you getting looser, coming undone.

I never really wanted to be free from you, but now that I was, I would have to build a home inside of myself, and I would never invite you in.

Acknowledgments

I would like to thank the following people:

This book began as my senior project at Bard College, written under the supervision of Mona Simpson. Without her, it would have been 120+ pages of nonsense. She is the best advisor one could imagine, and this book owes its existence to her patience and brilliance.

Mary Caponegro, an angel on earth, who opened doors for me that I didn't even know existed.

Shaye Areheart, who saved me from post-grad ennui and gave me to courage to send this story out into the world.

My teachers: Anne Carson, Paul LaFarge, Edie Meidav and Ann Lauterbach. I am honored to be in your debt.

Emily, Grace, Anastasia, Carly, Nick, Kedian, Mel and Sylvie, who lived with me during a pretty intense period of my life, and whose kindness, strength and humor kept me sane.

Elle Nash, the best editor a girl could wish for.

My parents, whose support is incredible and invaluable. Sorry I'm not going to law school.

Leah, my favorite reader.

My sister, the coolest person in the whole world.

I love you all more than I can say.

About the Author

Nicola Maye Goldberg is the author of the novel NOTHING CAN HURT YOU. She lives in New York City.

CPSIA information can be obtained
at www.ICGtesting.com
Printed in the USA
BVHW070013090223
658191BV00023B/705

9 781732 192003